"Sherwood concentrates on Celia's tart wit, the memorable supporting players . . . and the New Zealand locales. . . . The result is distinctively amusing throughout."

The Kirkus Reviews

"EXTRAORDINARY, WELL-DETAILED SETTINGS, A NICELY CONTRIVED POLITICAL ATMOSPHERE, AND GUTSY CHARACTERIZATION MAKE THIS MYSTERY WORTHY OF THE BEST OF NGAIO MARCH."

Booklist

About GREEN TRIGGER FINGERS

"Here's a midwinter pick-me-up for you gardeners. Not another seed catalog, but a village mystery about a lady horticulturist who digs up the most interesting things in the neighbors' gardens—including a corpse. John Sherwood has a charming amateur detective in Celia Grant."

The Cleveland Plain Dealer

Also by John Sherwood
Published by Ballantine Books:

GREEN TRIGGER FINGERS

A BOTANIST AT BAY

A Celia Grant Mystery

John Sherwood

BALLANTINE BOOKS • NEW YORK

Copyright © 1985 by John Sherwood

All rights reserved under International and Pan-American Copyright
Conventions. All rights reserved. No part of this book may be reproduced
in any form without the permission of the publisher. Published in the
United States of America by Ballantine Books, a division of Random
House, Inc., New York.

Library of Congress Catalog Card Number: 85-14519

ISBN 0-345-33023-4

This edition published by arrangement with Charles Scribner's Sons

Manufactured in the United States of America

First Ballantine Books Edition: October 1986

ACKNOWLEDGMENT

Most of the botanical information in this story is drawn from *Rare and Endangered Plants of New Zealand* by David R. Given (Wellington, 1981). Any lapses from accuracy are the author's own, but he gratefully acknowledges his indebtedness to Mr Given's authoritative book.

❧ ONE ❧

"Damnation," said Celia Grant as the outside bell of the telephone filled the cold December morning with its clamour.

Bill Wilkins dumped his employer's suitcase in the boot of the car. "Want me to answer it?"

"No, let it ring," she decided nervously. One never knew, the car might break down on the way to the airport.

"Oh Celia, you've lots of time," said Bill. "You don't want to wonder all the way to New Zealand who it was rang."

"Very well, find out. But whoever it is, I'm not here."

Having unlocked the house again and gone in, he did not hear. Celia looked at her watch and wondered how long she could stand the strain of pretending to be an unflappable long-distance traveller.

Bill opened the sitting-room window and poked his head out. "It's that Duchess."

1

"What d'you mean, 'that Duchess'?"

"Come off it Celia, you only know one."

"Oh bother, did you tell her I'm not here?"

"I said you was just leaving and I wasn't sure if I could catch you or not. Yes or no?"

Celia hesitated.

"It's urgent, she says, she must talk to you." He held the phone out through the window at her. "Wailing into it like a cat in love, poor woman, better put her out of her misery."

Not realizing what a fateful step this would prove to be, she took the phone from him. "Hullo Hermione?"

"Celia, thank goodness I caught you."

"I can only talk for a moment, my daughter's having a baby in New Zealand and I mustn't miss the plane."

"No dear, of course not," said the Duchess soothingly. "Which airport?"

"Gatwick."

"What's the flight number?"

Celia told her.

"Splendid Celia, I've a problem and I want to pick your brains, but I won't keep you now. We can talk at Gatwick, get there as soon as you can and I'll rush there hell for leather in the train from Victoria—"

"But Hermione—"

"—And tell you all about it while you're shuffling along in that nasty queue at the check-in. 'Bye now."

Tell me all about what, Celia wondered crossly as she snagged her tights on the bare thorns of a rose bush under the living-room window. She could guess the sort of problem and did not want to bother her head with anything of the kind just now, there was plenty to worry about without that. Bill Wilkins was a sound working gardener and conscientious but he was only twenty-three. Was it fair to leave him in charge of Archerscroft Nurseries while she shot off to the far side of the world? The business had grown with the move to new premises, there was almost an acre now of glass-houses and cold frames and seed beds. It was the slack season, but the offsets from the Archerscroft Strain of double primroses needed cosseting through the winter and there would be hell to pay if anything went wrong with the seedlings of *Helleborus* "Roger Grant", a prizewinning *corsicus x niger* hybrid which she had named in memory of her late husband. It had attracted a waiting list of privileged customers as long as your arm. She would be away two months, would Bill manage to sow the half-hardy annuals properly without her at his elbow?

"If you're ready, let's go," he said from behind the wheel.

She climbed in beside him, cursing herself for not having let the phone ring. After the bustle of last-minute jobs one had the right to relax when one finally got to the airport, she had been looking forward to it. The queue at the Air New Zealand check-in was no place for instant solutions to problems posed by the aristocracy, but Hermione was an old friend from when Roger was alive and a good customer, and would have to be listened to.

She spent most of the journey to Gatwick wondering if she had ordered enough *Viola cornuta* seed, but roused herself as Bill drove into the concrete wilderness surrounding the airport terminals.

"This will be the first time I've travelled so far without Roger," she said as they threaded the one-way traffic circuits of this monument to man's inhumanity to man.

"Oh Celia, you'll be okay. You know you only have to look helpless and six men will run to pick up your hanky."

This was exaggerated, but not wholly untrue. She was on the small side and slim, and her prematurely silver hair only served to set off a fresh complexion and features of Dresden china prettiness. Unfortunately men were often stimulated by this deceptively fragile display into becoming over-protective, and not all of them kept their baser urges to themselves. A few such nuisances would certainly be found in the economy class of a jumbo jet.

Bill wanted to park the car and see her off, but she dismissed him firmly as soon as he had deposited her and her suitcase at the kerb. He would have distracted Hermione's attention from explaining what was bothering her, for she felt it necessary to fascinate well-set-up young men and there would be no getting any sense out of her if she tried to do two things at once.

The Duchess was standing near the Air New Zealand desk, a little apart from the milling crowd waiting to check in. She saw Celia at once and waved, looking casually elegant as usual in very nondescript clothes. Their friendship dated back many years to the time when the Duke started restoring the eighteenth-century gardens at Melsingham and called in Roger to advise.

"Well done Celia dear, there you are. Put that

suitcase down here and we can kick it along as we move up the queue. Now listen carefully because this is important and we've very little time. You remember the Deed of Family Settlement?"

"Not really, no."

"The thing that Everard's grandfather lumbered us with because of death duties, in case people died in the wrong order."

Celia remembered vaguely now. Hermione and Everard often cursed the Sixth Duke, whose financial arrangements had made impossible rather than difficult the task of maintaining a 60-room Palladian mansion in Derbyshire with a leaky roof.

"And guess what else that crazy old man did, Celia. He smuggled as much lolly as he could out of the country to stop some long-forgotten Labour government from laying violent hands on it and he invested it guess where. Not foreseeing that the Thatcher woman would have the face to launch a thousand ships when the brouhaha started over the Falklands, he stashed the lot away in Argentina of all places. And now the Argies have turned nasty and won't send Everard a penny and our overdraft is astronomical and the bank is becoming hysterical . . ." While she went into more detail over her plight, Celia managed to dispose of her suitcase and secure a boarding card for a non-smoking seat.

". . . So to cut a long story short," Hermione ended, "we'll have the bailiffs in at Melsingham unless we can sell the Rembrandt."

"This is all very sad and I'm sorry," said Celia, "but I'm not good enough at finance to advise you and there's a huge hole in my tights and I want to pee and they'll start boarding any minute now."

"Never mind dear, planes never leave on time and you can pee and change your tights after you've been through the metal detector thing. As I was saying, our only hope is to sell the Rembrandt. But under this damnable Deed of Settlement we can't do that without Uncle Bertie's signature, and we've mislaid him."

Uncle Bertie, she explained, was the Seventh Duke's strong-minded but harum-scarum younger brother. The moronic heiress whom he had trapped into marriage had failed utterly to control him and despite his advancing years he still ran away from her at intervals with disreputable women.

"And now when we need him for once, he turns out to have done exactly that. His wretched Muriel, who has less intellectual curiosity than an earthworm, can't remember when she last saw him, whether it was a month ago or two. She's no idea where he is and only the vaguest about who he might be with. He'll probably turn up again sooner or later but we can't wait for that, he may have got himself killed by some jealous husband for all we know."

The "boarding" sign opposite Celia's flight began winking, but Hermione swept on. "It looks from what Muriel says as if the romance started in his greenhouse. A *femme fatale* came and fawned on him while he was repotting his *Raoulias*."

"*Raoulias?*" Celia echoed. "He grows alpines?"

"Yes dear, he takes things up. A few years ago it was breeding some extinct form of dog, and before that he gave the National Gallery hell for having the old varnish cleaned off the pictures, which he said ruined them. Nowadays it's rock plants. He wins prizes with them at that place in Vincent Square."

"But I know him!" cried Celia as it dawned on her that "Uncle Bertie" must be the dreaded Lord Albert Melton. "A tallish man with a round face and very thick glasses."

She could see him now, a moon-faced sixty-year-old, shouting and brandishing his walking stick in the middle of the New Horticultural Hall at one of the spring shows. He was scarlet with rage because of some grievance against the judges. This happened frequently, the committee was terrified of his capacity for making trouble. One confrontation with him had degenerated into a rough-house. Celia and a man from a Lincolnshire tulip firm had been detailed to take him out to lunch while means were found of preventing him from suing the committee for assault.

"Not the sort of person who eats out of one's hand," she added.

"Oh no dear, he'd bite off your fingers. Obstinate as a mule, too. Nothing will stop him turning out for the Melsingham shoot, frightfully dangerous. You're quite right, glasses like the bottoms of beer-mugs, and with them on he's still as blind as a bat. Everyone panics when he appears, even the dogs hide behind tree trunks without being told."

The "boarding" sign was still winking.

"Hermione, this is all very interesting but I must catch my plane."

"Very well dear, I'll come with you as far as the passport desk, but you haven't grasped the point." She scrabbled in her handbag. "Just take a look at these."

She handed Celia three photographs. They showed,

from various angles, an amply built woman with a great mane of red hair, lying stark naked on a settee with her eyes shut and smiling like a cat sated with cream.

"She looks like a woman in an advertisement who's fallen in love with the soap," said Celia.

"According to Muriel," said the Duchess, "this is the woman who fawned on Bertie in his greenhouse."

As a small concession to modesty the lady wore a spray of white flowers, tastefully lodged in her crotch.

"And there's this one," the Duchess added, producing a close-up of the flower spray and its immediate context. "Now Celia, look at that flower. I know I'm right, because Everard and I spent hours identifying it with a book. It's a Mount Cook Lily,* and don't you dare tell me it isn't."

Celia began to see the outlines of the trap she was being led into. She studied the picture. Leaves peltate, reticulate. Petals white, cuneate. There was no denying it, Hermione was right.

"And it only grows in New Zealand," said the Duchess.

"It is a New Zealand endemic, admittedly. That only means it doesn't occur anywhere else in the wild. But it could in someone's garden."

"No dear, I looked it up in all the catalogues, none of the specialist nurseries list it. And it should be in flower there now."

"Actually it starts flowering in late October, but it depends on the altitude. It gets later as you go higher up."

*The so-called Mount Cook Lily is in fact a buttercup, *Ranunculus lyallii*. It was named after Dr Lyall, the surgeon-naturalist on HMS *Acheron*, which surveyed the South Island coast of New Zealand in the 1840s.

"Anyway, Bertie must have taken that photograph in New Zealand in or since late October."

"How d'you know he took it?" Celia asked.

"Everard's been keeping an eye on the letter rack at his London club. These arrived two days ago in a folder containing his holiday snaps. The photographer says the reel of negatives arrived through the post with an open cheque and instructions to develop it and send the results to his club."

On thinking it over Celia decided that this arrangement was not really odd. Even the appalling Lord Albert Melton could hardly let starkers snaps of his lady-love be developed locally.

"Of course not, dear," said Hermione, "that's why Polaroid is such a success. Needless to say the envelope has been thrown away and they can't remember the postmark, but everything points to New Zealand, so—"

"Hermione, you do realize that New Zealand is the size of France and consists of two huge islands with a lot of sick-making water in between? You're not suggesting that I should ignore Lucy's baby when it emerges so that I can rush around looking for a red-headed nympho and asking her what she's done with Lord Albert Melton?"

"There can't be many red-headed nymphos in New Zealand called Rose Murphy."

"Is that her name? How d'you know?"

"Muriel says so, for what it's worth. She's not an intellectual giantess and I had to point out to her something she hadn't grasped, namely that Bertie always runs away with redheads, they're the only ones that turn him on. But she's positive that this one is called Rose Murphy and comes from what Muriel calls 'somewhere down there', being unable to distinguish between New Zealand and Australia. Here are the rest of Bertie's holiday snaps, have a look."

Celia took the folder. "Sydney Opera House isn't in New Zealand," she objected, picking one out.

"I know, he probably called there on his way. Look at these close-ups of plants."

The shots were all of alpines growing in the wild. Two of them were of celmisias.

"They grow in New Zealand," said Hermione. "Bertie went there two years ago and brought back some seed to grow in his greenhouse."

Celia remembered now. Celmisias were tricky, and Bertie had won commendations for his at the Horticultural Hall.

"So when I got your Christmas letter, dear, saying you were off to New Zealand, I remembered how clever you were about that corpse and that naughty old picture-faking lady, and I thought, what luck."

Celia had narrowly escaped with her life from the picture-faking episode. "With the best will in the world, Hermione—" she began, "I don't think—"

"Nonsense Celia, you're very clever, of course you can. Your son-in-law's in the Embassy there, except that in a Commonwealth country you have to call it a High Commission. Get him to use his influence."

But Jim Blakewell, Lucy's husband, had been in the Foreign Service less than three years, and was still the lowest form of organic life known to diplomacy. "I'd much rather you approached them officially," Celia said.

"We did, dear. Everard phoned the High Commis-

10

sioner, rather a common little man he thought, and he was very sniffy and unhelpful. Here, take Bertie's photos and this envelope—"

"But Hermione—"

"It's got a letter of credit in it for your expenses and some photos of him so that people can identify him—"

"No, really."

"And phone us to say how you get on. Goodbye dear, you'd better run along now and change your tights, you mustn't miss the plane."

"No, damn you, you're not rushing off like that. I want to know a lot more. Where did he meet this red-headed creature? Was she staying in the house?"

"No, in the village. In digs."

"What does the landlady know? Someone must go and tap the flow of gossip. Why the greenhouse? Did she just barge in there and if so what excuse did she give? When did he leave home, and did he go straight out to New Zealand from there or did he go somewhere with her first? He'd need a visa to get into Australia, what sort of visa and for how long? Did he get it before he left home, in which case the thing was planned in advance, or was it one of those last-minute impulses when you rush up to London to get the visa and hop into a plane? Find out all that and ring me at my son-in-law's in Wellington, here's the number. Good heavens, that's the last call. Goodbye Hermione, I must run."

❧ TWO ❧

When Celia changed planes at Auckland to fly on to Wellington she found that she was far less dilapidated than she had expected after the 29-hour flight from London. She had survived the barbarity of Los Angeles airport, the roast lamb which was mandatory on Air New Zealand, the mental confusion of crossing the dateline and the attentions of a young Danish businessman with wandering hands who clearly thought it very nice of him to be making a pass at a woman old enough to be his mother. Being small, she had slept comfortably despite the cramped conditions and had spent some of her waking hours studying Lord Albert Melton's holiday snaps.

He had certainly been in Australia. Apart from the Sydney Opera House he had photographed the Harbour Bridge and some street scenes with high-rise buildings, one of which included a bus labelled "Bondi Beach". Another series of pictures was of a rather comfortless village street at the foot of forbidding snow-capped mountains. Was this Bertie's New Zealand base for his excursions amid the flora of the Southern Alps? And who was the enormously fat man with a darkish beard posing on the verandah of a wooden house? Was the house in the same village?

The close-ups of alpines repaid study. Bertie was a surprisingly competent photographer of plants. He had taken several shots of each subject and the detail was often sharp enough for an identification, for which she was well equipped. She had no intention of coming all this way and seeing nothing but a clothesline filled with nappies, and would be off botanizing as soon as Lucy was properly back on her feet and knew one end of the baby from the other. She had therefore slipped a guide to the alpine flora of New Zealand into her hand baggage, intending to do her homework on the plane.

Thanks to the guide, she established that the two celmisias were *morganii* and *inaccessa*. A beautiful plant with pure white flowers proved to be a forget-me-not, *Myosotis colensoi*. There was also a whipcord Hebe with appressed leaves, impossible to identify without handling the plant itself, and a curious climbing daisy affair straggling through low bushes. The beauty queen of the collection was a tiny rock clematis, *C. marmoraria*, and the chief curiosity, if her identification was right, was a strange survivor from a pre-glacial era: a tiny buttercup crouching close to the ground, *Ranunculus paucifolius*.

If it really was *paucifolius* this was very interesting. It was listed as an endangered plant, but a widely publicized rescue operation had made it well known in international conservation circles. It was known as the

Castle Hill Buttercup, and its range was limited to Castle Hill, wherever that might be. And Bertie had gone there to photograph it.

When, though? Ten days or a fortnight ago if the book was right; it was in flower in the picture, which meant mid-November at the earliest. Before or after the visit to Australia? Maddeningly, the reel of negatives had been cut into strips in the laboratory. One of the strips had all the Australian pictures on it, but there was no knowing whether this came before or after the flowers and the fat man with the beard and the village street. Perhaps if one looked at the cuts in the negative through a microscope one could match the edges and arrange the strips in the right order. . . .

Another point. Bertie seemed to have concentrated on plants with a limited distribution, often confined to a single area. *Celmisia morganii* grew only in the north-west corner of South Island and *C. inaccessa*, true to its name, in the inaccessible mountains at the other end. The hebe and the straggling daisy-thing were still a mystery but Castle Hill, the only place where the buttercup clung to its precarious life, was miles from there in Otago, with the white forget-me-not as a neighbour. Bertie must have moved fast to photograph all these while they were in flower. Why rush around like that? What had these particular plants in common to make him seek them out?

The plane reached the southern end of North Island and circled over Wellington, ready to land. Celia realized with a shock that Bertie's affairs were not what she ought to be thinking about. She put the photos away and made herself concentrate on her role as a grandmother-to-be, which would be full-time for at least a month. It was infuriating, here were the makings of a lovely little problem and she could do nothing about it. To satisfy Hermione she would prod the High Commission into making a few routine enquiries, but even if they came up with anything interesting she would be far too busy to follow it up. Fastening her seat belt moodily, she thrust from her the thought that Lucy's forthcoming baby was really rather a nuisance.

"Muriel? Hermione here. Have you done what I told you?"

"No, I decided it was too undignified. Going down to the village and gossiping with the tradespeople about that woman."

"Damn it, Muriel, you don't deserve to have any dignity, it's shockingly careless of you to mislay Bertie just when he's wanted. Have you at least found out where the Murphy creature was staying?"

"I expect it was at that bed-and-breakfast place."

"Didn't you make sure?"

"No, Hermione, I couldn't bring myself to."

"Oh dear, you really are a fool. The whole village knows that Bertie behaves like a randy tomcat on hot bricks when he sees a redhead he fancies, why pretend you're too stupid to have noticed?"

"Bertie hates being spied on."

"This time he'll have to lump it. I shall drive over tomorrow and interrogate all and sundry about his horrid little odalisque."

"It's all so sordid, Hermione."

"Not as sordid as me and Everard begging in the streets while the roof at Melsingham falls in on the bailiffs. See you tomorrow."

Sunshine. Blue water almost up to the edge of the runway. A modest airport building and in front of it, waving excitedly, Jim Blakewell, Celia's nice ugly son-in-law, and Lucy.

"Aren't I enormous?" said Lucy amid hugs. "I can't wait to get it out of my system."

"I know dear, the last weeks are awful, one feels like a constipated jellyfish."

"She behaves more like a dog," said Jim. "When nothing interesting's happening she curls up in her basket and goes to sleep."

"I went to sleep in my last relaxation class," said Lucy. "The woman gave me hell."

On the drive into town there was much to ask and much to take in: wooden houses, a hugh landlocked harbour, boats, and on the shore a pair of black and white wading birds of devastating beauty.

"Oh, what are they?" Celia asked.

"Pied stilts," said Lucy and went on discussing the merits of different types of pram. This topic lasted until Jim drew into the kerb outside an alarmingly sordid apartment block surrounded by a concrete garden wall. This was covered with graffiti praising love and marijuana and abusing someone called Piggy, who seemed from the context to be a politician. "The police are an organized crime," Celia read. "Wreck the fascist tour. The treaty is a parody of a fraud of a shambles of a parody." What tour? What treaty?

"This is the university quarter," Jim explained. "It's all right, we live opposite."

Celia studied the graffiti. "But I thought New

Zealand consisted of sheep and a few healthy-minded male Bo-Peeps to look after them."

Jim gave her one of his charming jug-eared grins. "Not any more. The Age of Innocence is over. This is the Age of Sex, Drugs, Unemployment, Immigration and the Colour Problem."

"But there isn't supposed to be a colour problem here."

"So everyone complacently thought. I'll tell you about that later. Come on in."

He showed her into a large weatherboarded house with an ornate Victorian-style porch. It was divided into flats, and theirs was hot, and small for three. Celia wondered if she should have come. Her offer to come had been a guarded hint, had they taken it up for fear of hurting her feelings?

Beyond the living-room was a large balcony with an awning over it. Celia stepped out, and checked back an exclamation of dismay. During the drive from the airport she had been too absorbed to notice that they were climbing. The house was clinging to a precipice and the balustrade was not child-proof. A toddler with any initiative would lose no time in dashing its brains out on the roof of the next block, 50 feet below.

All around, office blocks and houses were clinging to the steep slope down to the water. Whoever chose Wellington as the nation's capital had failed to notice that, although its natural harbour was magnificent, there was nowhere next to it where anyone in their senses would attempt to build a town.

"Coffee," Lucy decreed, and Celia went with her to help get it. They had so much to say to each other that half an hour passed before they went back to the balcony, where Jim had tactfully remained out of earshot of obstetrical enquiries. Over the coffee, however, Celia decided to get Hermione off her conscience by mentioning the problem of Bertie.

Jim pulled a long face. "Lord Albert Melton is a wingeing pom." Celia looked puzzled, and he added: "A wingeing pom is a person from the United Kingdom who never ceases to complain in a loud whine about aspects of this country's arrangements which displease him."

"Bertie doesn't whine, he shouts," Celia corrected, remembering the Horticultural Hall.

"He also uses expressions like 'down under', which implies that there's something wrong with the Southern Hemisphere, and 'Australasia', which implies a close connection between New Zealand and her bullying barbaric neighbour, whose one idea is to grind New Zealand's face in the mud. Furthermore, he is a self-important nuisance who thinks he ought to be wined and dined by the High Commissioner and made a VIP fuss of whenever he chooses to come here."

"Is that often?" Celia asked.

"He was through here two years ago and at least once before that. He comes plant collecting and botanical circles dread him."

"He's supposed to be here now, why hasn't he contacted the High Commission and asked to be made a fuss of?"

"Goodness knows, but he hasn't," said Jim. "There was something about him the other day, though. I can't remember what."

"The Duke rang your head of mission, who was unhelpful for reasons I now understand."

"Oh yes, he wanted us to get an SOS message put out on the radio for him. But BCNZ won't do that unless there's a relative dying. Wanting to flog off a Rembrandt isn't an emergency."

"Jim dear, can't the immigration people help? You have to fill in a form when you arrive. If there's one for him we'll at least know he's here."

"The problem would be to find it. They only bother about overstayers, their forms surface when they ought to have left. When did he arrive? That might help."

"I don't know. Hermione's trying to find out when he left England. Perhaps he could be traced through the lady in the case. Her name's Rose Murphy."

"Not *the* Rose Murphy?"

"I don't know. Is there one?"

"On second thoughts it couldn't be. She's a very serious left-wing lady, romping with a lord wouldn't be her style."

"I've some photos of his Rose Murphy here," said Celia. "Rather striking, don't you think?"

Jim eyed the red hair and glorious expanses of white flesh and whistled admiringly.

"Hey, that's enough of that," said Lucy, reaching for the pictures. "Really Mum, you're here to keep my husband calm, put them away." About to hand them over, she did a double take. "Jim love, it *is* her. It's Red Rosie."

"It can't be."

"Look at her *face*, you lecherous idiot."

"Good Lord, so it is. How odd." He turned to Celia. "I don't believe it. Rose Murphy is a respectable dyed-in-the-wool pillar of the New Zealand Labour Party."

"Oh? Then what is she doing stripping off and teasing an elderly aristocrat with that saucy nosegay?"

"Photos can be faked," Lucy suggested.

"I doubt it, Lucy love, you'd need special facilities. These were processed in the normal way along with the rest of the reel."

Jim explained that Red Rosie was the combative left-wing MP for one of the North Island industrial towns. Her husband had held the seat before her, and she had taken his place at the by-election caused by his death. "He killed himself," Jim added. "There was a scandal, something about a girl who was under age and had a baby. It wrecked his political career and he shot himself in a boat he had, he couldn't stand the shame. Rose swears he was framed and never stops saying so."

"And was he?"

"It's possible. The far right here does a very skilful line in character assassination, they've got rid of one or two inconvenient left-wingers that way." He picked up the photos again. "This beats me. Politicians are weird enough with their clothes on, naked they're unthinkable."

"Perhaps she can explain what she was up to. If she's an MP someone in Wellington must know where she is. Could the High Commission find out?"

He rose. "I'll try when I get to the office, which is where I ought to be now."

"She may even be in Wellington herself."

"Not in the summer recess."

The summer recess, Celia thought. In December.

And this balcony, which faces south, is deliciously cool and shady. I must remember that everything is the other way round, tender plants need the shelter of a nice warm north wall.

"I'm sorry to bother you with this," she said as Jim left. "Hermione and Everard are good customers of mine, and they're going mad with worry."

"And you, my dear mother-in-law, will go mad with curiosity until you know the answer."

Over drinks before dinner that evening he reported the result of his enquiries. "I rang the Canterbury Alpine Plant Society in Christchurch. Lord Albert hasn't contacted them but they sounded horrified at the mere suggestion that he might be around. The immigration people say nothing doing till we can give them an approximate date of arrival, but I have found out about Rose Murphy. She's in South Island, campaigning against a hydro-electric dam that the government wants to build."

"What's that to do with her?" asked Lucy. "Her stamping ground's up north."

"Ted Murphy was born down there, at a place called Kirkstone where his parents kept the general store. If the dam's built it will submerge his home township, so she's there creating hell about it. Perhaps she regards his birthplace as a sort of shrine."

Trying not to sound too interested, Celia said: "Where is this home town of his?"

"I'll get a map. It isn't a town though, more like a hamlet. You don't talk about 'villages' here, that's a word with 'ye olde' associations, they're all called townships. Just as they're all 'paddocks', not fields or meadows. In the country you even play rugby in a paddock."

"Dear me, I must go to evening classes and learn the language."

He unfolded the map. "Here's Kirkstone, right up in the mountains at the lower end of the Kirkstone valley, which the government wants to flood. You'll have a job getting there."

"Oh no, Jim. I'm not budging from here. Besides, how d'you know she'll be there?"

"Sure to be, the news agencies say there's a big meeting there about the dam, press and TV invited, the lot. It's the day after tomorrow, you'll have to fly down to Christchurch and hire a car, but if you want to ask her why she treated Lord Albert to that bold floral display, here's your chance."

"I can't go, Lucy needs me."

"Oh yes you can, and I don't," said Lucy firmly. "Jim and I talked it over and made up our minds. I shan't hatch out for at least a week, and meanwhile I'm not having you sitting here half dead with curiosity and wishing you were in Kirkstone."

"But I ought to be finding out where you keep the ironing board and how temperamental the oven is."

"Nonsense," said Jim, handing her an envelope. She took it. "What's this?"

"Your ticket to Christchurch on the afternoon plane tomorrow."

The road followed the river up the valley through a thick forest of dark-green trees with tiny round leaves, which Celia did not recognize. The road was well engineered, with long stretches of tarmac, but driving

22

was an effort. Because the tourist season had begun, the only vehicle available for hire in Christchurch was an unwieldy camper with berths and equipment for four, and it had taken most of the morning to find that. Its steering was leaden and its thirst for petrol tremendous.

The valley narrowed into a gorge, with the river she had been following for 50 miles thundering down it. At a warning notice "Seal Ends" the tarmac stopped and gave way to loose chippings the size of potatoes, whereupon the road began winding upwards steeply in dizzy hairpin bends. Having encountered similar conditions lower down, Celia flung the camper forward boldly, with the rear wheels skidding slightly at every bend. At the top of the gorge a wide tussock-grass valley opened out, surrounded by hills. They had the scalped look of country that had been cleared of trees to create sheep runs, and snow mountains loomed high behind them. Celia felt and was very high up. She rounded a bend, and crossed the river on a one-track wooden bridge. There, at the foot of a formidable mountain, was a low huddle of buildings: Kirkstone.

She parked behind a huge tourist coach, and her first impression was that this tiny isolated settlement was inhabited only by Japanese. But Kirkstone was at the foot of a pass over the Central Alps to the scenic delights of the west coast, and the tour operators found a "comfort stop" necessary before this leg of the journey. Presently the Japanese, who had been making full use of the café and public lavatory provided for their benefit, piled back into their coach and were driven away, gazing out with inscrutable envy at the wide open spaces so lacking at home in Japan.

The departure of the coach left the street un-populated and Kirkstone temporarily bereft of its apparent reason for existence. But Celia, taking stock, saw that it was also what her guidebook called a service township, which supplied the basic needs of a widely scattered farming community. There was a garage which probably repaired farm machinery as well. The general store looked as if it sold sheep dip and fencing wire as well as food. Less material needs were catered for by a simple wooden church and schoolhouse.

More to the point, Kirkstone was recognizable at once as the street scene in Uncle Bertie's holiday snaps. The general store and garage were in the right places and the garage sold the right brand of petrol. The war memorial at the end of the street had the right design of cross, and the church was right too. This was a nice surprise, but where was everybody? There were cars and farmers' utilities parked everywhere, the meeting about the hydro-electric scheme must have begun. She explored. A gaunt two-storey build-ing described itself as "Brown's Hotel" and was obviously a pub, but seemed to be shut. The Sunny-bank Motel, in the yard behind Crampton's general store, consisted of five motel units with no public room. She investigated a rough track leading off the main street between Brown's Hotel and the school, and discovered rugby goalposts. But the track con-tinued past the end of the pitch and seemed to lead to a corrugated iron structure with dogs tied up outside, from which faint sounds of oratory could be heard. She hurried towards it and squeezed her way into a crowded building which common sense and a strong smell of sheep identified for her as a woolshed.

With a little manoeuvring and polite pushing through the people standing at the back she found a place where she could get a clear view. The dignitaries were up on the shearing platform facing the crowd. They were surrounded by media razzamatazz, with photographers prowling about ostentatiously and TV crews holding up hot lights. A wall map entitled "Kirkstone Valley Hydro-Electric Scheme" hung behind them.

A prosperous-looking man with flamboyant grey sideburns was in full flood of oratory. Sitting next to his empty chair was the red-haired but fully clothed original of Uncle Bertie's studies in the nude. Even in a sweater and skirt with her hair anyhow she was a strikingly handsome woman and she knew how to use her looks. With a varied repertoire of facial expressions denoting bewilderment she was making it amusingly clear that she could not make sense of what the man with the sideburns was saying, let alone agree with it. She was deliberately making the audience restive, and presently there was an interruption from the floor, which he handled with the assurance of a practised politician. Celia asked her neighbour who he was.

"That's our member of parliament, Trevor Thornhill of Mount Ephraim."

The audience was clearly dissatisfied with what he was saying, but had not become noisy. Celia had been wondering why, but this explained it. A member of parliament in the thinly populated South Island was an awesome potentate, whose electorate covered a huge

25

territory. He wielded extensive patronage and was not a man to offend.

An elderly farmer speaking from the floor followed him, and made it clear to Celia what the issues were. The hydro-electric dam would create a huge artificial lake stretching 30 miles or more up the Kirkstone Valley, submerging some farms and depriving others of the winter pasture on the valley floor which made them viable. The township would disappear and the new lake would be a big obstacle to getting supplies in and livestock out to market. The compensation would be miserly. A long-established community would be scattered to the four winds, to scratch a living where it could. As usual, South Island was being exploited to provide electricity for the feckless townees of the north.

Thornhill rose to reply, but the meeting was getting heated. The main outcry came from a group of young people, led by a blond youth with a thin, nervy face, and from a striking-looking girl with dark hair and eyes, but some of their elders, perhaps seeing safety in numbers, began to join in. The words flew, and enriched Celia's vocabulary. "Duck shoving" was the local name for buck-passing between government departments. A "Queen Street farmer" was a city slicker who owned land or stock for tax-fiddle reasons. "Skite" and "drongo" were terms of abuse. A "cow-cockie" was a dairy farmer and inferior for some reason to a "runholder" concerned only with sheep. A "piker" was a faint-hearted person who gave up the fight too soon, and according to the blond young man and his companions Trevor Thornhill was a piker because he was arguing against taking the fight against the dam to the high court: another threatened community had spent every penny they possessed on legal fees, and look, Thornhill said, where it had got them. The right course now was to try to extract maximum compensation from the government.

He tried to add something about the need to "think big" and plan for industrial development, but the youngsters set up a massive shout of "hypocrite", in which part of the audience joined. Thornhill replied by calling them yobbos and warning them that they would be chucked out of the meeting unless they stopped yahooing about. Trouble threatened, and a group of solid-looking farmers sitting near the platform bestirred themselves for action, but Rosie stood up and raised a hand. This produced silence at once. The yobbos, it seemed, were the Red Rosie fan club.

She was standing between Thornhill and a boxlike contraption, no doubt the wool press. Instead of starting to speak she looked first left at the wool press, then right at Thornhill, then left again with a glint in her eye which invited the meeting to share the joke. A slow chuckle swelled into a guffaw as the allusion sank in. In one of New Zealand's best-known detective stories the corpse of a member of parliament was stuffed in a wool press and discovered weeks later in a bale of merino on its way to auction.

"Good on you, Rosie, stuff the bugger in," shouted the fair-haired cheer-leader of the yobbos. The dark girl beside him scowled fiercely.

Rosie held up her hand again and started to speak. "Well folks, we know what Trev here is on about, eh? We didn't come down in the last shower, we know our Trev. Don't fight the government, he says, let them flood your land, let them take away your livelihood, I'm not putting my hand in my pocket to pitch in for a fighting fund. I'm okay, he says, my fifteen thousand acres are way up on Mount Ephraim at the head of the valley, I'm not getting my feet wet in this damn lake. While you drown I'll be away laughing."

There was a gasp from the audience. Rosie, the left-wing outsider from the north, had mentioned the unmentionable. This was the issue that had kept the meeting rumbling with discontent and thanks to her it was out in the open. But why had the protests been so muted till now? There must be some hidden reason.

"Well folks, I have news for you," Rosie went on. "Trev is right when he says don't waste your money, don't mess around with the law. He's right because he knows it's heads I win, tails you lose, he knows that the lousy National Party Government he supports will change the law if what the law says doesn't suit it—and that will go on till it has to face the voters and gets what's coming to it. But we're not piking out, there are other ways we can defend ourselves. I'm glad to see so many media people here, because I'm about to show you proof that the New Zealand Government will commit a brutal ecological crime if it goes ahead with this dam."

She looked into the audience. "Where's Joe Marano?"

A clean-faced young man with glasses and a prominent Adam's apple stood up.

"Ah, there you are Joe. Come up here where we can all see you . . . that's better. . . . Joe here, folks, is a talented young botanist on the staff of Massey University. The other day I suddenly wondered what bits of botany our clever government was going to drown under its two-hundred-million-dollar dam, so I asked Joe to fossick around a bit. He came up with quite some discoveries, and I'd like you to hear what he found. Joe Marano.''

A polite round of applause. Thornhill's face was a study in surprise and baffled fury. Rosie had snatched control of the meeting away from him and there was no way he could get it back.

Marano launched into his subject with the zest and authority of a specialist. Most of the Kirkstone Valley, he said, was without interest botanically because the flora had been destroyed by grazing or by competition with introduced plants. But in its upper reaches the river ran through a series of gorges with steep sides, inaccessible to grazing animals. This area was rich in botanical interest. For the moment he would ignore beautiful species growing there like the Mount Cook Lily and the commoner celmisias, which were widespread in the Southern Alps, though the destruction of yet another habitat in which they were found would be a crying shame. But he had also found a number of species so rare that their threatened destruction was a matter for serious international concern. Could he have the first slide please?

Someone at the back of the woolshed switched on a projector. Rosie turned the wall map of the hydroelectric scheme back to front, so that its white back could be used as a screen. All this had clearly been well rehearsed. Almost at once a picture of a plant flashed on to it.

'Helichrysum dimorphum,'' said Marano. "This species is down to less than a hundred plants, because

29

in 1978 they sprayed a gorge rather like yours from the air to stop the gorse spreading and destroyed the only big population of the helichrysum that we know of. There are one or two small colonies elsewhere, but it's listed as 'endangered' and the discovery of half a dozen plants in your valley is very reassuring and encouraging. Next slide please.''

This was riveting. Marano's *Helichrysum dimorphum* was none other than the straggling daisy-thing that Celia had failed to identify in Bertie's photos, and more surprises were to come. He went on to deliver brief illustrated lectures on *Celmisia morganii*, which was listed as rare, and *C. inaccessa*, which had hitherto been regarded as local to its wet mountain fastness in the far south. Their discovery so far from other known populations was again a matter of some importance, as also was that of next slide please, *Myosotis colensoi*, a charming white forget-me-not which he had also found and which was listed as endangered. Next slide please.

This, he declared, was the rare *Hebe poppelwellii*.Celia was prepared to take his word for it, all whipcord hebes looked more or less alike to her. There was no proof that it was the one in Bertie's pictures, but any doubt about that was swept away when Marano produced his star turn and focus of conservationist concern, the Castle Hill Buttercup. The discovery of no less than ten plants at a site several hundred miles from Castle Hill was an event, he said, of enormous scientific importance.

It was also an event which had spared Bertie the need to rush to Castle Hill with his camera. All the rarities he had photographed had been sitting waiting for him at the top end of the Kirkstone Valley.

Marano went on to talk at rather too great length about less rare species that he had found, then launched into a vehement but repetitive condemnation of the government's ecological barbarity. Rosie evidently thought this had gone on long enough and interrupted.

"A question, Joe. These plants are all under threat, right?"

"Too right, Rosie, they are. People might dig them up for their gardens, that's why I'm not giving the exact locations. Or they can be killed by indiscriminate spraying, like the helichrysum."

"You hear that?" cried Rosie. "But it's all organized, from tomorrow we'll have volunteers keeping a dawn-to-dusk watch on that gorge, so if the government think they can spray the ecological evidence away and build their dam, they can think again."

This was too much for Thornhill. "You wash your mouth out, Rosie," he began. "That's a foul thing to say." The yobbos drowned him out with shouts of "shuddup" and "siddown".

"Now let's consider this thing calmly," Thornhill yelled. But this was what the yobbos were determined to prevent. They surged forward to the shearing platform and tried to drag Thornhill off it.

"Stop that now, you little bastards," shouted Rosie. "We'll have no violence here."

This too was ignored. Two solid farmers who had already shown their support for Thornhill came forward as his defenders and a fight started, half on and half off the platform. The blond young man had seized a chair and was using it as a weapon. One of the farmers tried to get it away from him. Between them they managed to bash Thornhill in the face with it. His nose began to bleed.

"The meeting's over, clear the room!" Thornhill shouted, dripping blood. His two farmer supporters took up the call. Several other men joined them to form a cordon, and they advanced down the wool-shed, shepherding the people out. They muttered angrily but went.

Meanwhile Celia was watching events on the shearing platform. Rosie was dissociating herself from the violence of her supporters by a display of concern for Thornhill's bleeding nose, and had whipped out a large white handkerchief to give to him. He clapped it to his face, then realized whose it was and handed it back to her.

"Oh no you don't, you snoopy bitch," he cried. "You keep away from me."

Celia was fated to puzzle for hours over the bizarre scene which followed. One of the men had given Thornhill a red bandana which he was holding to his face. All that could be seen of him was a pair of horror-stricken eyes and the sideburns. He was staring at the other handkerchief, the white one spotted with blood that he had just handed back to Rose Murphy. She was staring back at him, blank with amazement. It was as if some enormous revelation had burst on her, making her forget the handkerchief which hung limply from her hand.

"Hey, give me that," cried Thornhill, trying to snatch at it. But she drew back sharply and stuffed it into her handbag.

For a moment it looked as if he would attack her, but he thought better of it. "Let me get out of here," he muttered. Crashing down from the shearing platform, he hurried out of the woolshed.

Rosie shook off what looked like a trance and started to hold court for the media men who were converging on her. ". . . Yes, an all-out campaign on a worldwide scale. . . . The biggest ecological scandal since Tasmania. David Bellamy? Sure, and any international body willing to help. A TV interview? Certainly, but will you excuse me if I do the radio one first, it's for the morning bulletins."

The newspaper men put their questions and went. As the group round her dwindled in size, she noticed Celia hovering on the edge of it. "Hullo there, who are you?" she asked, but her shrewd politician's eyes amplified the question: who are you and what use can you be to me?

"I'm Celia Grant. From England."

Oho, said the cold shrewd eyes in the smiling face, I can certainly use you. "You're press?"

"No. A . . . botanist. I have a question or two I'd like to ask you."

Rosie gestured towards the TV crew, apologizing for having to give them priority. "I'm having a bit of knees-up at my house tonight for the visiting botanists, Celia. Do come, why don't you? We can have a real talk there."

"How kind. I'd like to."

"You have somewhere to sleep?"

"A camper. It's parked in the street."

"Drive it into the yard behind my house. You'll be quieter there. See you in about an hour."

Celia thanked her and went. At the door of the woolshed she turned for a last look at the shearing platform. Had that extraordinary little drama really been played out on it, or had she imagined the whole thing? What did it mean?

❧ THREE ❧

"Now Muriel, make a real effort to concentrate. You must remember when he packed up and left."

"I don't, Hermione. I keep telling you."

"Let me try to jog your memory. What time of day, morning or evening?"

"Evening. Yes, I came down to dinner and he wasn't here and Evans told me he'd gone up to London."

"Then he was here at lunch time?"

"I suppose so. I don't really remember, it was just an ordinary day."

"Oh dear. This is his desk, isn't it? I shall go through it, there may be some clue."

"It's locked. Bertie hates me to interfere with his things."

"Damn, if it wasn't by William Kent I'd bust it open. What's this great pile of letters?"

That's where Evans puts his mail."

"Then these are what came after he went missing. What are we waiting for, let's look at the dates on the postmarks and we'll know where we are. Mostly November, but—yes, a few at the end of October. This is the earliest, it was posted in Glasgow on the seventeenth of October."

"Oh. You mean, he must have gone away before that."

"No, Muriel dear. It's got a second-class stamp and the post office sits on those for ages to teach us not to be mean, it could have been ten days in the post. You're mad not to have opened his mail, give me that paperknife."

"Oh Hermione, do you think you should?"

"Yes. One of them may say 'in reply to your esteemed communication of the twentieth of October . . . ' and if he was here writing esteemed communications on that date he can't have been in New Zealand at the same time. Bills. Begging letters. Boy Scouts, but he never went in for that, thank God. What's this? The Obituary Editor of The Times thanks Lord Albert Melton but regrets that for reasons of space, etcetera. Someone must have died and he wrote to The Times."

"Oh! Oh Hermione!"

"Good God, Muriel, what's wrong? Are you ill?"

"No! I've remembered! That was on the day he went."

"Go on. Who did he write to The Times about?"

"Oh, I don't remember that."

"Can't have been anyone important if they didn't print it."

"They had printed something and Bertie read it and thought it wasn't enough and wrote some more."

"I know the sort of thing: 'If I may add a footnote to your admirable tribute to my dear friend Lord X, only his closest intimates knew of his lifelong interest in ladies' underwear.' But who was it about? Concentrate, Muriel. Man or woman?"

"Man . . . I think."

"Oh, this is hopeless. I shall go to the village now and pick up what gossip I can about his redhead, and tomorrow I shall bring you The Times *for the last fortnight of October. And you will put a cold towel round your head and read all the obituaries till you find a name that looks vaguely familiar. We will then know when your husband left home."*

"I'll try, but I don't remember much about it, except—"

"Yes?"

"When Bertie saw that this person was dead, I think he was rather excited."

Celia had taken up Rosie Murphy's suggestion and driven the camper into her yard. The house was on the main street opposite the general store which had once belonged to her husband's parents and his grandparents before them. Its most noticeable architectural feature was the porch on which Bertie had photographed the fat man with the beard.

When she joined the party, the big farmhouse-type kitchen was full of people and dirty plates and beer cans. Rosie was working hard, darting about among her guests and keeping everyone in play like a chess master taking on 20 opponents at once. Apart from the blond young man and his yobbos most of those present were botanists who had come from a distance at

Rosie's invitation to be present at the unveiling of her rarities and help guard them.

While Celia waited for the "real talk" she had been promised, she chatted them up and discovered that New Zealand was in a state of ecological as well as socio-political turmoil. The dreaded gorse was not the only introduced nuisance spreading too freely, for instance buddleia and privet were proliferating everywhere like a science fiction nightmare. Escaped garden plants and introduced weeds were colonizing waste land and the stern and wild Mackenzie country was overrun with wild roses and tourist coaches and heavy traffic to and from the hydro-electric schemes. The native bird life had suffered from nest-robbing magpies and mynah birds, which had "got in from Australia", the source, it seemed, of most ecological evil. Meanwhile the native flora was itself evolving and throwing up new hybrids all the time.

Several aspects of the rarities puzzled Celia greatly, and she asked Marano why they had not been spotted and recorded earlier.

"No one had looked at the Kirkstone Valley," he explained. "There are so many places to explore, so much that hasn't been recorded. The other day a man came in with a daisy from the Marlborough mountains that no one had seen before. It's a race against time getting it all on record before it's destroyed."

Deciding that he had given her as much of his time as she was worth, he cast around for a way of getting rid of her and picked out for the purpose an old man with very pink cheeks and very bright blue eyes who was sitting by himself, apparently stupefied by the noise. "I'd like to introduce Tom MacRae to you, Mrs. Grant."

"I'd be delighted, but tell me about him first."

"He's a retired doctor who made a lifelong hobby of botany, like your Keble Martin or Gilbert White, a real old identity. Come on over."

He made the introduction and slipped away. Celia cast around for an opening gambit. "Tell me, what is an 'old identity'?"

Dr MacRae grinned. "An elderly bore with a non-stop flow of reminiscences, mostly untrue. Did that feller say I was one?"

"Yes, but he meant it as a recommendation."

"You're from Britain. You like New Zealand?"

"The scenery's wonderful, and I've never seen such splendid trees, but I'm bewildered by the flora. I picnicked at midday in a field of poppies that looked familiar, and it took me ages to realize that they were eschscholzias escaped from someone's garden."

"Funny way of teaching people how to spell your boyfriend's name correctly," said Tom MacRae. A twinkle of the blue eyes showed that this was meant as a challenge.

Celia decided to bring up her heavy artillery. "I know, and it didn't work, the beautiful young Friedrich Eschscholz always gets an extra 't'. Chamisia* would have been better. Kotzebuia would have been dreadful, though."

A repeat of the twinkle showed that she had passed her test with credit. She asked him what he thought of Marano's rarities.

Eschscholzia californica was named by Adelbert von Chamiso on Captain Otto von Kotzebue's expedition to California in 1815. Dr Eschscholz was a handsome young naturalist and physician attached to the expedition. Chamiso was attached to him.

He looked at her with a curious expression. "Ecology's odd here, things happen fast. The Monarch butterfly was pretty rare till this fad caught on and a Swan Plant covered with Monarch caterpillars, that's what they feed on, became a conservationist status symbol."

Celia was about to point out that he had avoided answering her question, but was interrupted by two women called Amy and Clara, who had already given her a great deal of unwanted information about distant relatives of theirs "back home" in England. Their voices were loud and their laughs an unnerving screech uttered without warning. Tom MacRae had fled in horror. She looked round for means of escape and caught Rosie's eye.

"Hi Celia," said Rosie. "You having fun?"

Celia assured her that she was, and asked on a note of casual social enquiry if Rosie could give her news of Lord Albert Melton.

Rosie frowned in an effort to concentrate. She was rather drunk, Celia realized.

"Dear Albert, you know him, do you Celia? How is he?"

"Haven't you seen him? He's supposed to be in New Zealand."

The frown deepened. "No, is he? I haven't heard from him since I was in Europe earlier this year."

"But surely—" Celia began. To her fury Amy and Clara chose this moment to close in again and set up a clamour to the effect that they were having wonderful fun and meeting such interesting people. Rosie dealt with this efficiently and turned to go, but Celia pursued her. "One moment, Mrs Murphy."

"Oh call me Rosie for God's sake, everyone does."

Her speech was a little slurred. There was no hope of getting sense out of her in this state and at a party too, where interruptions came ten a minute.

"Perhaps we could have a real talk tomorrow?" she suggested.

"Oh that's right, Celia, I forgot to say. Joe Marano's taking the first shift of volunteers up the gorge in the morning to guard the plants so they're not trampled by sightseers. You can go with them and write it up for the British press."

"But I'm not a journalist. I really wanted a long talk with you."

"Oh, I shall be up that way too. See you tomorrow, it's a date."

This was unsatisfactory, but nothing could be done. Rosie could not be confronted at her own party with nude photographs of herself as evidence that she was lying. With luck she would have forgotten her stupid falsehood in the morning and make more sense.

The party had been going on for hours, and showed no signs of abating. Celia had gathered that the visiting botanists were to doss down in the house, and the yobbos, who were holding a separate party of their own in a corner, had brought their bedrolls in with them for the same purpose. There were five of them, the dark girl, the fair-haired cheer-leader, a youth with brown eyes and red hair, and two other young men. Throughout the evening they had mixed with nobody, but now a sudden disturbance and shouting broke out in their corner. Everyone turned to look. The fair-haired young man had got Joe Marano against the wall and was punching him in the stomach.

Rosie advanced towards him. "Bazzer, you little drongo, what the hell d'you think you're doing?"

Bazzer let Marano slump to the floor and turned. "You asked for it Rosie, it's your damn fault."

Rosie was swaying a little on her feet, but her speech was clear. "Out. The lot of you, out. You've done enough harm already this evening. I want you out of here."

Suddenly Bazzer was in a towering rage and clowning at the same time. "Oh Rosie, forgive us, what have we done? Have we made a blue?"

The other three male yobbos sniggered unpleasantly. The dark girl maintained a sullen mask of disgust.

"Harm? What can she mean? Oh Rosie, I'm so distressed and embarrassed, I don't understand."

His pale face was pinched and hysterical. He was deliberately acting up to annoy her.

"Trust you far lefties to trivialize any cause you muscle in on," Rosie stormed, "and make it disreputable."

"You mean, because we went rude at Thornhill and broke up the meeting? That was good tactics, the media were there."

"Yes Rosie," said one of the male yobbos, sniggering. "You have to demonstrate to the media that your uncontrollable anger at fascist oppression is uncontrollable."

Bazzer nudged him viciously. For him this was no joking matter.

"Out, all five of you," Rosie decreed. "After that crappy exhibition you have the nerve to beat up one of my guests. Out, you're not spending the night here."

"Damn you!" shouted Bazzer, trembling with anger. "Who begged us to come all the way from Auckland to buck in and give you a hand? Who carried on like a slag to make sure we'd come?"

The party stopped in its tracks. After a moment Rosie said in a small, taut voice: "You better go now if you want to get out of here alive."

Bazzer did not move. Two tough-looking botany students from Canterbury University walked up to him. One of them said: "You want your face re-arranged?"

"You heard what the lady said, piss off," added the other.

The dark, scowling girl spoke for the first time. "Don't act silly, Bazzer. Come away."

Bazzer reassembled what remained of his dignity. With an imperious toss of his fair hair, he led his followers out.

The party took a little time to gather momentum again after this disturbing incident. Celia found herself pinned against the wall by an elderly woman who told her a long ecological horror story about some conservationists who had landed on a small offshore islet and shot the wild goats which infested it, so that the scrub which they had grazed to extinction could regenerate. The parakeets which also inhabited the islet had sampled the corpses, found that goat was to their taste, become carnivorous and attacked the limpets on the shore when the supply of goat failed. "So the ecological balance will be distorted by the seeds that the parakeets don't eat," the lady concluded. The fate of the goats did not, it seemed, distress her.

"They should have cut off the goats' beards and exported them to Germany," her husband added, "for Bavarians to put in their hats. They fetch good prices there."

New Zealand, he added, was in desperate need of exports. With Europe and America dumping agricultural surpluses at rock bottom prices, New Zealand lamb had to be slaughtered islamically and bartered for Iranian oil. Chinese gooseberries, marketed as "Kiwi Fruit", were the latest hope, but they were being over-produced. . . . Celia listened with genuine sympathy, but she was dropping with fatigue. The party showed no signs of ending, so she decided to escape.

Out in the yard behind the house it was pitch dark. But why were the lights on in her camper and the curtains drawn? She pulled open the door.

"Hi there, princess," said Bazzer.

All four men were there, sitting on her bunk and smoking. But not pot, she decided after an experimental sniff.

"How did you get in?" she demanded.

"That padlock is a piss in the hand, princess, when you know how."

"What a disgusting expression. Will you go now, or shall I get some men from the party to throw you out?"

"Now don't get your underwear in a twist, princess," said Bazzer in a sexy drawl. This was alarming. He was clearly a role-playing fantasist. For the moment he believed in himself as an all-conquering macho male.

"Hey fellers, this sheila's a beaut," he proclaimed in an outlandish backwoods accent. "We've picked ourselves a yummy bit of crumpet without knowing it."

One of the other yobbos slid along the bunk towards the door, ready to grab her if she turned and ran. The party was still going on in the house. Would anyone hear her above the noise if she shouted for help?

"Very stale crumpet," she said as lightly as possible. "You wouldn't enjoy it."

"But princess," he drawled, "us sex-starved bushwhackers buried out here in the sticks have to make do with what we can get."

"Queen Street bushwhackers from a commune in Auckland, more likely. Come on, let's relax. I'm sure you don't talk like a milk-bar cowboy at the commune."

He frowned angrily. "You talk like a pommy."

"I am a pommy."

Bazzer clapped his hands hysterically. "Hell's bells and buggy wheels, a real pommy princess from the darling old cobwebby Yuke Kay. How long have you been in godzone?"

"Godzone. Is that a Maori expression?"

"Godzone country, princess, is our proud name for complacent, fascist-governed New bloody Zealand."

"I shouldn't get too depressed about it, Bazzer. It's no worse than anywhere else I know, and the scenery's much better."

"But here they think it's the only country worth living in and everywhere else is hell," said Bazzer as his accent went rapidly up-market.

"Really? I thought you were all beginning to realize that life everywhere is rather complicated."

"Life is damnably complicated," Bazzer agreed. "There's a theory that if anyone discovers what the world is for and finds out the meaning of life, then it will instantly be replaced by something even more complicated and bizarre. However, there's another theory which says that this has already happened."

"That sounds like something that intellectuals write on walls. Is it original, or have you been reading graffiti?"

Bazzer broke into a broad grin. "Hey, I like you," he said.

"I like you too, and I'd love to talk politics some more in the morning. But I've had a long day and it's my bedtime."

"Fine. We can go on talking in bed."

"Oh dear, must I take your threats of rape seriously? I'm old enough to be your mother."

"How d'you know I'm not mother-fixated like the unfortunate Mr Oedipus?"

"He ended up blinded, so look out. I suppose the idea was to frighten me into letting the four of you sleep in here?"

"Why not? Rosie threw us out in the cold and this is a big camper. Remember what Lenin said, to each according to his need."

"Well, my need is to have you out of here."

"Selfish, I call that. A total misreading of Lenin's teaching."

"I'll share it with some women if there are any without beds, not with four lusty young rapists."

A jokey conversation developed, with both sides on edge. Bazzer was no longer trying to frighten her, but obviously saw no way of withdrawing from the camper without losing face with his silent associates. She tried chatting them up, and had some success with two of them, whose names proved to be Andy and Reg.

But the red-haired youth with brown eyes remained fierce and silent, as if still hoping for rape. Struggling against sleep, she talked on and tried in vain to think up a face-saving formula for Bazzer. The deadlock threatened to go on all night.

Relief came in the form of an angry female voice shouting "Bazzer! Bazzer!" out in the yard.

Before anyone else could react Celia opened the camper's door. "He's in here."

The dark scowling girl who had been with him at Rosie's and in the woolshed appeared out in the darkness.

"*Kia ora*, Jessie," said Bazzer. "Come in and join the party."

"What the heck are you doing in here?" Jessie asked crossly.

"Only talking," said Celia. "But it's bedtime now and I was just saying, if there are any women without a bed there are some spare bunks in here. How about you?"

"Why thanks, I'd be grateful," said Jessie, relaxing into a smile.

But this did not suit Bazzer. To judge from his expression she was his girlfriend and he proposed to assert his extra-conjugal rights.

"Hey, I want to talk to you," he said, gripping her arm.

She pulled herself away. Bazzer and his three acolytes hurried out after her into the night, which filled at once with the harsh echoes of his quarrel with Jessie. The voices soon faded away into the distance and Celia took out Bertie's photographs. A problem connected with them had been worrying her all evening, and she had to try to solve it before she slept.

Bertie had photographed all the plants mentioned by Marano in his lecture to the meeting in the woolshed, and also one other which Marano had failed to mention: the charming little cream and white *Clematis marmoraria*. She located it on the strips of negative. It came between the helichrysum and the forget-me-not. Had Bertie wandered off to some other part of the alps after snapping the helichrysum, photographed the clematis, and returned to the Kirkstone Valley to do the forget-me-not? Surely not, the clematis must be growing somewhere in the area that Marano had searched for rarities, and it was certainly rare. Why had he not mentioned it? If he compared notes with Bertie he must have known it was there.

As she thought about possible explanations there was a knock on the door. Jessie was outside clutching a bedroll.

"*Kia ora*," she said.

"What does that mean?" Celia asked, letting her in.

"It's a Maori greeting, but *pakehas* use it too. It makes them feel good about respecting our culture."

"You're a Maori, then?"

"Three quarters of one. When you've been here

longer you'll be able to tell at once. We have these curly mouths and by *pakeha* standards our legs are too short for our bodies, but we like it that way. Thank you for letting me sleep here. I need a rest from Bazzer."

"He can be tiresome, I imagine."

"Too right he can, and I'm exhausted. That meeting was a drag, as if anyone cares what happens to this place."

"Are you saying that fighting the Kirkstone Valley dam isn't an important issue for you?"

"Right again, it's a sideshow," said Jessie harshly. "I kept telling the others that South Island is dead, hardly anyone lives here, even the sheep would vote for that damn National Party if they knew how. There's no Maoris here, not enough to get up a bit of steam over the race problem."

"But everyone says New Zealand doesn't have a race problem."

"Don't let the *pakehas* brainwash you. They're polite to us and they pretend to admire our carving and our dancing and our sweet nonsensical folk legends, why? So they don't feel guilty about taking our land and keeping all the good jobs for themselves so that we take to crime to live. All the time we're here I feel guilty because I'm not up north campaigning against the Treaty."

What was this about a treaty? Celia foresaw that the explanation would be long and passionate, and put a different question. "In that case, why did you come?"

Jessie's dark features froze in a moment of blank silence. Celia felt instinctively that the blankness covered confusion over some issue which could not be discussed frankly. Whatever answer she got would be a half-truth at best.

"You heard what Bazzer said to Rosie," Jessie replied after the silence had lasted a long time.

"If I understood rightly, he accused her of behaving like a whore to make sure he'd come."

"That's right, and it was true. She dragged him here by the short and curlies, but he shouldn't have said so in front of all those people."

"Why did she want him here? And the rest of you?"

The wooden expression which masked confusion appeared again. "His behaviour at the meeting wasn't very helpful," Celia prompted.

"He overdid it, that was her fault, serve her right. She thought she'd got herself a tame supporters' club, but when Bazzer got here he had a nasty surprise, the lover-boy situation wasn't vacant anymore. When he made for the bedroom there was someone else ahead of him in the queue. Joe Marano had to be persuaded to do something that Rosie wanted, so he was getting the treatment instead. Bazzer was furious and ran amok at the meeting. That was why he started beating up Marano at the party."

This came off the tongue easily. Jessie had talked her way out of the area of embarrassment, whatever it was.

"What did she want Marano to do?" Celia asked.

"Anyone's guess."

"But Jessie, this seems an extraordinary way for a serious politician to carry on. Getting men to further one's political aims by promiscuous behaviour."

50

"She started to be this way after her husband died, that knocked her right off balance. You know about him?"

"Only that there was a sex scandal and he killed himself."

"That's right, the girl was under age and there was a baby. When the story broke he knew it was the end of his career in politics, so he put a shotgun in his mouth one day in his boat and pulled the trigger. Rosie tells everyone he was framed, but she doesn't believe it."

"Oh? How d'you know?"

"Look at her behaviour. She reasons this way, if Ted Murphy was unfaithful to me, what the hell does it matter if I shag with all and sundry? It's not that she likes it, Bazzer says she has to get very drunk first."

Celia remembered the strange, happy look on Rosie's face in Bertie's nude pictures of her. This explained it. They had been taken without her knowledge when she was very, very drunk.

"I can just imagine," she said, "that a woman might behave like this in pursuit of some all-important aim."

"Too right," said Jessie. "That's why she's doing it."

"To save Kirkstone from drowning under a lake? If she regards her husband's birthplace as a sort of shrine—"

"Hell no, she's not fussed about that. She hated the place, never came here if she could help it till now. All she cares about is avenging her husband. How? By getting the dam stopped and making Trevor Thornhill look a fool because he said it couldn't be done. Why

Trevor Thornhill? Because he was the one who broke the story of the sex scandal, sounded off to the Prime Minister and the press with all the juicy details. The way Rosie looks at it, Thornhill killed her husband.''

❧ FOUR ❧

Some time during the night Celia was woken by a whispered argument at the other end of the camper. "Why not? . . . What's the point if we don't. After coming all the damn way from Auckland? Be your age, Bazzer. Just because she went crook at you . . . what d'you expect if you go shagging with a nympho grandma?"

The camper bounced a little on its springs as someone moved about, presumably Bazzer trying to get into bed with Jessie. Celia wondered drowsily whether to throw water over him as one would to cool the lusts of an intruding tomcat, but went back to sleep instead and had an unpleasant dream, in which she was a saxifrage and potbound. Her roots were being squashed agonizingly in a two-inch pot, and no one realized that she needed potting on into something larger, though they kept tapping her pot to see if she needed water . . . she woke. Someone was tapping on the window of the camper.

"Who's there?"

"Joe Marano. Rosie said you'd like to come up the gorge with us. We start in half an hour, okay?"

It was still dark and not at all okay, but if this was the only way of getting Rosie to herself, so be it. She switched on the light. Jessie's bunk was empty and her bedding was gone, she must have accepted the hospitality of Bazzer's bedroll elsewhere. Celia dressed quickly, had coffee and cornflakes, and stuffed a rudimentary picnic into the pockets of her parka. Equipped with a botanical field guide, a large-scale map and Bertie's photographs, she stepped out into the chilly air.

Dawn was just breaking. Marano was waiting in front of Rosie's house by a minibus. When he opened the door for her to get in a shock wave of noise hit her as Amy and Clara greeted her like a dawn chorus of peahens. Before they could insist on her sitting with them she dumped herself down at the very back beside Tom MacRae, who was looking healthy and distinguished in an endearingly battered felt hat. She was delighted to see him. A detached observer who knew the New Zealand flora well was just the person whose brains she needed to pick about the queries that Marano's rarities had raised in her mind. She intended to fascinate him at the earliest opportunity, but he had shrunk away from her into his corner with an alarmed expression, as if afraid that she would add her quota to Amy and Clara's uncivilized noise. She took a temporary vow of silence, to lull him into a false sense of security. Presently she would exude sticky substances like a fly-catching *Drosera longifolia* and trap him.

Rosie's front door opened. Three sleepy botany students who had been at the party came out and climbed into the minibus. Marano started the engine.

"Isn't Mrs Murphy coming with us?" Celia asked.

"She'll be along later," said Marano and drove off.

Curses, thought Celia. Why had she not checked? Here she was being hustled out into the bleak dawn to botanize in the company of two screeching female lunatics while Rosie lolled in bed recovering from last night's party. A golden opportunity had been missed. A KGB-style invasion of the bedroom and a little brutality would have made any woman with a hangover tell the truth.

Just outside the township, where the main road headed up to the pass, Marano branched off it along an unsealed road which kept to the valley floor. To Celia's bad-tempered eye it was a boring valley, with sides worn smooth by some ice-age glacier and heavily grazed. There was not a presentable flower in sight. Amy and Clara were still screeching to each other and anyone who would listen. Presently they produced a bag of sweets and passed it round. Tom MacRae declined with polite horror and Celia followed his example. During the brief silence enforced by chewing she asked Marano where the road led to.

"It ends at the Mount Ephraim Station, that's forty miles on. The roads to the Derwent and Mount Shelley Stations lead off it too."

"They're all sheep stations?" she asked.

"No. Mount Shelley's a government cattle breeding establishment and Derwent's a deer ranch, that's a government scheme too. Wild deer are too destructive, the policy now is to farm them. Venison's become quite an important export."

After 20 bumpy miles the valley began to narrow, with clumps of the Mount Cook Lily along the banks of the river. This was better, there were steep rocky slopes protected from grazing animals and already she could see two sorts of celmisia flowering in damp, shady rock crevices. She decided to be less bad-tempered. The delay in confronting Rosie was infuriating but nothing could be done about it, so she might as well enjoy the New Zealand flora.

Presently Marano halted the minibus and everyone got out. "There's the helichrysum," he said, pointing, "in front of that patch of gorse."

The valley had narrowed into a gorge. The colony consisted of half a dozen plants, straggling through low scrub on the steep slope down to the water. Celia stepped down from the road to get a better view.

"Keep back, please," said Marano. "And when the sightseers come, will everyone please make them keep back too. If the ground's all trampled round the sites, it'll be obvious where they are, and we'll have people digging them up for their gardens in no time."

"Not if they're guarded, surely?" Celia objected.

"We can only keep watch for a few days. After the publicity we've given these finds, people will be coming up here for months. And the tragedy is, unskilled transplanting kills them."

From Marano's point of view the object of the

expedition was to post his morning shift of sentries. Celia's aims were more complex: to pounce on Rosie as soon as she appeared, which according to Marano would be any time now; to solve the mystery of the *Clematis marmoraria* which Marano had failed to find, and various other mysteries about his discovery which had occurred to her; to cultivate Tom MacRae (avoiding guilt by association with Amy and Clara) and pick his brains; to identify if possible the actual plants photographed by Bertie, thus proving that his pictures had been taken here and nowhere else; and to avoid being distracted from her other aims by a wealth of beautiful but not rare plants which she had never seen before.

There was no hope, though, of matching any of the helichrysums with Bertie's photos, which had been taken early in the flowering season. Now it was well advanced, bringing with it growth and change under the influence of sun and wind. When the minibus halted again further up the gorge the same proved true of the little whipcord hebe. But she was luckier with the *Celmisia inaccessa*, one of a largish colony growing in the crevices of a rock face dripping with water. Plants might grow and wilt, but rock did not change and the limestone crevice in the picture was unmistakable.

The beautiful white forget-me-not had colonized a limestone scree with a rock in the middle which also figured in the photos. But matching plants to pictures was no longer Celia's main concern, and she made no attempt to do so at the next stop, at the Castle Hill Buttercup. Normally she would have been fascinated by this botanical celebrity with its bright yellow flowers and strange little leaves, but she was being forced to a conclusion beside which the problem of the photos was insignificant, like ladders in one's pantyhose during an earthquake; a conclusion she disliked very much.

The *Celmisia morganii* was the last of the rarities and the nearest to the top of the gorge. Of the original party only Celia and Tom MacRae remained to admire it, the others had been left on watch lower down. While Marano turned the minibus for the journey back to the township, they stood studying it on a high bluff above the road. Celia stared at the wilting daisyflowers and ripening seedheads, looking for something she knew was not there. There was only one word for *Celmisia morganii*. It was embarrassing.

MacRae was searching too, leaning far forward to poke about delicately with the tip of his walking stick among the lance-shaped leaves of the celmisia.

"There aren't any, are there?" she said. It was the first time she had spoken to him since the expedition started.

He looked at her in panic, horrified either by her unladylike forwardness in addressing him, or by the implications of her remark. She moved away and sat down on a rock to check altitudes on her map. Several minutes passed. Then a shadow fell across the map. MacRae was looking down at her from under the battered felt hat with an alarmed expression.

"What did you mean, 'there aren't any'?" he barked.

"There are no seedlings. There should be."

He nodded, as startled as she was at having to think the unthinkable. He began to speak, but his voice was drowned by the deafening racket of a helicopter which appeared suddenly from somewhere down the gorge, passed low overhead, and flashed away towards the heights of Mount Ephraim.

"Ed? What's the situation, report please."

"The minibus is parked about two hundred yards down the gorge from the Mount Ephraim cattle grid. There's a man standing beside it, and a woman sitting on a rock about fifty yards from the road, with a man standing beside her."

"There were eight people in the minibus when it left the township. Where are the others?"

"It looks as if the minibus dropped them off one by one further down the gorge. There's a man near the Shelley Station turnoff, and two women a mile below the one to Mount Shelley."

"Then these are the naturalists mounting guard, it's part of this publicity campaign of Red Rosie's."

"Then one of the women by the Mount Shelley turnoff must be her."

"No, according to the township she left there on a trail bike twenty minutes ago. Look Ed, I'm not fussed about the botanists, I reckon they're just cover for the other thing. It's the kids that broke up the meeting that we need to watch. Any sign of them?"

"Nope."

'They drive a clapped-out Ford Transit. Make another pass up the gorge and see if you can spot it."

"Will do. 'Bye now."

"What was it *doing*, flying so low?" Celia asked indignantly.

"Who can tell?" replied MacRae. "In these degenerate days some people even use them instead of dogs to muster sheep."

Their eyes met. After a moment's hesitation, Celia returned to their problem. "There should be seedlings," she insisted. "According to the book *Celmisia morganii* flowers freely in the wild and produces numerous seedlings, and it's supposed to form 'erect tufts, often massed into large groups festooning bluffs and ledges'. It hasn't. All the plants are roughly the same age, two or three years old, and they haven't been here long enough to produce any seedlings. They're cultivated plants reintroduced into the wild."

"Yes. Yes," he said. As a further mark of approval he sat down beside her.

"The altitudes are wrong too," she went on. "The hebe belongs up above the tree-line. The book says it sometimes comes down into herbfield, but surely not as low as this? The same applies to *Celmisia inaccessa*, it couldn't possibly come downhill as it travelled north from Fiordland. *Morganii*'s all wrong here too, it's a lowland plant."

"Never believe what the books say about height," said MacRae.

"I know, I kept telling myself that, but the celmisias and the hebes and the forget-me-nots are all youngish, there are no old-established clumps at the centre of the colonies to produce all these two- and three-year-old plants. And how did the Castle Hill Buttercup get here? It belongs miles away, with a very limited range. It's obvious, they wanted to publish a list of rarities threatened by the dam, and they decided it would have far more impact if New Zealand's best-known plant at risk was on it. This whole ecological thing is a forgery, and a rather clumsy one."

"Ed? Report in please. What's the situation now. Where's Rosie got to on that trail bike?"

"Just passing the Mount Shelley turnoff and coming up fast."

"Listen Ed, the township says someone heard the kids' Transit start up and drive off long before dawn. You're sure you've not seen it?"

"No. If they started that early, they could be way up on Mount Ephraim by now."

"Not unless they busted down the gate over the cattle grid. I had it padlocked last night."

"It looked okay ten minutes ago."

"They could have found the Taranake Gate* and got in that way. Make a sweep over Mount Ephraim and see if you can spot them."

"Okay if you say so, but ten to one they've hidden the Transit away by now under the trees."

The helicopter clattered away, and disappeared above the beech forest which overhung the top of the gorge. Normal conversation became possible again.

"You've thought about the difficulties, Celia?" MacRae asked.

They were on first-name terms now, and Celia had

---

*A short length of wire fencing which can be dismantled to form an unobtrusive gate.

decided that he was the most delightful old gentleman she had ever met. They were kindred spirits. He was as full of adrenaline as she was at the prospect of a mystery to solve.

"Growing them wouldn't be impossible," she said. "The celmisias would be tricky, the book say *morganii* sulks in cultivation and won't set seed, and you have to grow *inaccessa* under a dripping tap and feed it with regular doses of crushed lime. I don't know about the hebe, but the helichrysum strikes easily from cuttings and the buttercup and the forget-me-not can be cultivated from seed. A skilled grower could do it."

"Have to gaze into his crystal ball first," MacRae objected. His blue eyes twinkled with enjoyment at making things difficult. "The timetable," he prompted.

"Oh. Yes, I see what you mean. When was it first known that the Kirkstone Valley was threatened with this dam?"

"Early last year."

"And these are three-year-old plants, which he wouldn't have grown because he didn't know they'd be needed. But he could have bought them from specialist growers."

"They'd blow the whistle and declare a foul when they saw where their plants had ended up."

"Even if they were paid a lot of money to keep quiet?"

"Sure, those fellers are too respectable. University botany departments and the like, they'd grow them and perhaps a few private enthusiasts. They all know each other, it would be too risky. None of them would lend himself to a Mary's Meadow stunt."

Mary's Meadow. A Victorian children's book about a girl who planted out cowslips from a garden in a farmer's field. He really did enjoy making things difficult.

"But saving this valley's a good ecological cause," she argued. "There are lovely things growing here apart from the rarities, so called. Any botanist would want to save it."

"Not this way, botanists have consciences and the conservation code's strict, like the Ten Commandments." He glowered comically from under the battered hat. "Thou shalt damn well not introduce cultivated plants into wild habitats without first getting the approval of the appropriate authorities, and even then thou shalt introduce only specimens grown from locally derived materials, to avoid genetic contamination."

"Suppose the grower was abroad, Tom. In England, say." It was an absurd idea, but Bertie must fit somehow into this shocking botanical charade.

"No. The seeds are tricky, a lot of them won't germinate unless they're absolutely fresh. Put them in the post and they'd be dead as mutton before he could sow them. He gets over that headache, then he brings the plants here. The Agriculture Department faints with horror and burns them at the port of entry for fear of plague and pestilence."

"They could be smuggled," Celia said, but had trouble imagining Bertie smuggling plastic bags of temperamental alpines through the Auckland customs.

And what state would they be in after the long journey from England?

"Another snag," said MacRae. "When's spring in Britain? April. May. They'd have flowered."

"Oh! Dear me yes, they'd be resting."

"That's right. Wave your magic wand till you're blue in the face, nothing would make them flower again here in November-December."

"But they *are* cultivated plants," Celia insisted.

"Must be. Marano's only a postgraduate student. Even so, you'd think he'd notice."

"Rosie has been exerting her charms on him."

"Ah." The blue eyes twinkled. "They say she kicks up her heels, did she kick them up at him?"

"So I'm told. Love, and the hope of making his reputation with a sensational discovery, may have made him careless. Anyone with experience wouldn't have been fooled."

"That's what foxes me, Celia. Whoever fixed this up knew enough to get hold of some very fancy plants, but not enough to realize that the experts wouldn't be fooled."

"Or else he knew the set-up would look suspicious, but reckoned the experts would keep their doubts to themselves once the conservationist bandwagon got rolling to save the valley. It's a difficult bandwagon to put into reverse, must we?"

"I think so, yes."

"Thank goodness you're here, I couldn't face it alone."

"Pure chance. I thought someone should look at this gorge before it was flooded, so I came and found the job had been done."

"Not very well. Must we really blow the whistle and declare a foul?"

MacRae hesitated. "When we get back to the township I'll phone one or two cobbers of mine, get them to come and have a look-see. A few second opinions from people with academic standing would give us moral support."

The helicopter was coming back, its noise got louder every moment. Down by the minibus Marano, who had spent the last half-hour eating a copious mid-morning snack, was pointing down the gorge and shouting something. Just before the helicopter's racket blotted out all other sound, Celia caught the words "Here's Rosie."

"Harry? There's no sign of the kids' Transit, and Rosie's almost at the minibus. Shall I return to base?"

"No, I want to know what Rosie does when she stops at the top of the gorge."

'Okay, but I can't hang around here much longer, they'll realize they're being spied on."

"Then go away and frig about somewhere for five or ten minutes, then make one more pass to see if she goes anywhere near the Mount Ephraim gate."

The helicopter was right overhead, its noise was frightful. And up out of the gorge came a rival source of noise, a huge, dusty motorcycle with very fat tires, ridden by Rosie in a bright-red parka. She drew level with Marano and paused to shout something to him without stopping the engine. Then ignoring Celia, she rode straight on.

"Hey! Stop!" Celia shouted as Rosie roared away past her.

The trail bike halted 50 yards on up the road. Rosie waited there for Celia to catch up.

"I'm sorry, I forgot," she said. "You had something you wanted to ask me." Her smile was a political masterpiece. I am deeply interested in your concerns, it said, but please be brief because I'm in a hurry.

"It's about Lord Albert Melton," Celia began.

"What about him? I told you last night, I haven't seen him since I left Britain."

"I'm afraid that isn't true."

The political smile vanished. "You need to watch your mouth, my dear."

"He took these photographs of you," said Celia, and held them up for her to see, one by one.

Rosie stared in deep shock at her naked, drunken self and tried to speak. Only a harsh, meaningless noise came out. Celia was deeply embarrassed for her.

"They were taken on your living-room sofa," she said. "I recognized the pattern on the upholstery."

Rosie struggled for speech for a long time. "You little scrubber. Accepting my hospitality and spying on me."

"I think you're allowed to spy on your hostess if she tells you lies."

Rosie climbed off the trail bike, propped it up and turned to face Celia. "Bertie Melton is the worst pain in the ass I ever met, but my dealings with him are no damn concern of yours or anyone else's except mine."

"Quite, but may we discuss this calmly? I'm not

concerned with your morals, they're entirely your own affair. All I want to know is where he can be contacted. His family need to get in touch."

But there was no calming her, she was beside herself with anger and confusion. "What else have you got in there?" she asked, staring at the photographer's wallet in Celia's hand.

"Pictures of all your rarities, taken soon after they were planted out. And one of a *Clematis marmoraria* that you had to keep quiet about because it died after it was transplanted from its pot."

Rosie stared at her, breathing hard. "Those photos were not taken by Bertie Melton, but by someone quite different. They were stolen from me and I want them back."

The attack was sudden, but Celia had been expecting it and threw the folder away out of reach as Rosie grabbed at it. Rosie made for the folder. Celia shot out a foot and tripped her, then seized her by the ankle to prevent her getting back on her feet. Rosie kicked herself free, stood up and charged. Compared with Celia she was huge and heavy, it was like being hit by a bull. Never underestimate the power of a woman, Celia thought, as she lay breathless on the turf.

While Rosie went for the photos Celia attacked the motorcycle and pushed it over to delay Rosie's escape. As it lay on its side with the wheels spinning Rosie came back. Celia pushed her over on it and grabbed at the red parka, determined to get the photos back as Rosie lay entangled in hot metal. But again, Rosie was too strong for her and landed a rabbit-punch which knocked the breath out of Celia. In a moment she had righted the trail bike, mounted it and ridden away up the hill.

But not far. Instead of fading away into the distance the exhaust noise stopped abruptly. Rosie must have cut the engine, somewhere just over the brow of the hill. Celia picked herself up and panted up the road in pursuit. Reaching the brow of the hill, she saw what was delaying Rosie. A hundred yards ahead the road was blocked by a gate with a notice on it reading: "Mount Ephraim Station, keep out." Rosie had propped the trail bike on its stand and was trying to open the gate. Unsuccessfully. She gave up the attempt, pushed her mount out of sight into the scrub and climbed over, to go on up the road on foot.

Celia hurried up to the gate. It was padlocked. Beyond it the road plunged into a dark forest of native beech trees. A formidably high fence stretched along the forest edge to either side of the gate. The gate was over a cattle grid, in which Celia trapped her foot, and had barbed wire along the top. She scrambled over it somehow and hurried after Rosie.

There was a bend a few yards beyond the gate. After that the road ran straight for a stretch, but there was no sign of Rosie ahead. However fast she walked she could not have gone on out of sight yet. But a narrow side-track led steeply downwards off the road, and a flash of red among the tree trunks showed where she had gone. Celia plunged down the track after her, making as little noise as possible, and was rewarded from time to time by a flash of red parka among the trees ahead.

Rosie was walking very fast, it was difficult to keep

up with her. Twice Celia had to choose at random when the path forked and Rosie was out of sight, and she was soon forced to the conclusion that she had chosen wrong. The feebly traced path she had been following led down to the river at a point where it was too fast and deep to cross, and did not start again on the other side. She had been following a maze of tracks made by animals coming down to the river to drink, and she was lost.

What to do? Follow the river downstream? That would merely lead her to the formidable wire fence, at an unknown distance from the gate. It would be better to work her way uphill again till she struck the road.

By now the sun ought to be in the north or thereabouts and she had a map. But the thick canopy of leaves made it difficult to see where the sun was. Luckily there was little undergrowth, but tumbled rocks covered with moss made movement difficult. She was not really frightened, but saw now why the early settlers had disliked the native bush, calling it gloomy and boring, and had destroyed huge areas of it as quickly as possible.

An hour's strenuous wandering brought her no nearer the road. She sat down to rest and eat her picnic before deciding what to do next. While she ate she wondered. Was Rosie telling the truth when she said Bertie had stolen the compromising roll of film from her? He was quite capable of it. If he had, the whole problem would have to be rethought from a fresh angle.

"Ed? I'm worried. We've had a man watching the Mount Ephraim road since noon. Rosie's not come up

it, she must have turned off somewhere. Her trail bike's still down by the gate, she must still be somewhere on Mount Ephraim land."

"Why panic, Harry? Without transport she won't get far enough to do much harm."

"But what's she after? How much does she know? I hate the thought of her loose on the Mount Ephraim run and us not knowing where she's got to."

"Think we ought to find her?"

"Yes. Come over here and we'll organize it."

Celia was very tired. The sun was getting low. She had found a road of sorts and tried to walk south on it. But the road wound about through the bush and she was forced to conclude that it was not the road which led up the gorge to Mount Ephraim. In places it was a mere track, barely passable for vehicles, and it was not marked on her map.

But it had to lead somewhere and she trudged on. She had been resting for the regulation ten minutes in every hour, and it was time to rest now. But as she sat down on a fallen tree trunk she came to another uncomfortable conclusion. The vague crackling noise she had heard in the bush to her left was not an echo of her own footsteps as she had hopefully tried to believe. It was still going on, not very far away.

About to call out "Is anyone there?" she thought better of it, for fear of attracting the attention of some hostile animal crashing about in the undergrowth. A wild pig, for instance, a descendant of the pigs released by Captain Cook, historically interesting as evidence of what an eighteenth-century pig was like, but was an eighteenth-century pig fierce? To judge by the noise at least three of its descendants were advancing towards her up the slope. It would be prudent to climb into a tree.

Having done so she peered down through its branches. The noise came stealthily closer and revealed its source as human. Five men were advancing in line abreast like beaters at a pheasant shoot.

"Good evening," she said as one of them passed underneath her.

A scowling face looked up. "Hey fellers, here she is. You coming down, Rosie you crazy bitch, or shall I come up and get you?"

"Don't bother, I'll come down," said Celia. "But I'm not that crazy bitch Rosie."

The scowl deepened. "Oh hell, nor you are."

"Listen Mr Marano, you just don't treat a nationally known TV interviewer this way. Where is Mrs Murphy?"

"I'm sorry, I have no idea. When she passed me in the gorge she said she was going up to Mount Ephraim, but—"

"Hell, we set up an in-depth interview for a prime evening slot, and she's an hour late."

"Something must have happened. She's very punctual keeping appointments as a rule."

"When you do see her, tell her we've gone back to Christchurch, and don't ring us, we'll ring you."

"Where does this road lead to?" Celia asked as the driver of the Landrover followed the windings of the road she had trudged along for hours.

"Nowhere much. It's just a forestry track."

But there were no stands of *Pinus radiata* or any other commercial timber. This was mixed primary forest; would it yield enough usable lumber to justify road-making on this scale?

Of the five men in the Landrover she recognized two as among the solid farmers who had supported Thornhill at the meeting in the woolshed. One of them, Ed Moffat, was driving. He was a dark young man with gipsy-style good looks and patches of hair left unshaven on high cheekbones. On her other side on the front seat was Harry Watson, a gloomy heavyweight with a big belly and a pompous manner to match. The three men in the back seemed to be of inferior status, hired hands perhaps. They had been introduced by their first names only, and a not-before-the-servants atmosphere had developed when she tried to find out why a full-scale manhunt had been mounted for Rosie.

"We'll talk when we get back to the Station," said Watson curtly.

Moffat engaged the four-wheel drive and swung the Landrover abruptly off the track and into the bush. After much bumping over rough ground and dodging among the trees he came out on what proved to be the Mount Ephraim road, less than a mile above the locked gate.

"Short cut," he explained. "Saves quite a lot of mileage."

Why explain, Celia wondered, unless something has to be explained away? What had registered with her was that the Landrover had transferred itself from a mysterious road system which had no obvious purpose and was not marked on her map, and on to one which was. Moreover, there seemed to be no connecting road between them.

Watson unlocked the gate at the cattle grid and opened it for Moffat to drive through. Rosie's trail bike was still there, half-hidden in the scrub. Watson gave it a dirty look as he climbed back into his seat, and muttered something to Moffat that Celia did not catch. There was no sign of Marano, the minibus or the sightseers who had presumably been gaping at the rarities. It would be dark in a few minutes, no doubt everyone had gone home.

At the turnoff to Mount Shelley, Moffat braked. "We go to your place?"

"No, yours," said Watson, and gestured towards the hired hands in the back. "Their transport's there."

Moffat nodded. A few miles further down the gorge he turned off on to the Derwent Station track. It climbed steeply up the side of the gorge and out on to a wide plain of tussock grassland, with a shelter belt of trees round a farmstead in the distance. The track led to the only break in the shelter belt, where a gate labelled "Department of Agriculture and Fisheries, Derwent Experimental Deer Ranch" opened into an area where high wire fences, like the one on the Mount Ephraim boundary, enclosed paddocks containing herds of red and fallow deer. The rotors of a helicopter could be seen above a low range of wooden buildings.

"So the helicopter's yours," said Celia.

"We use it to locate wild deer and trap them," Moffat explained.

A utility was standing in the yard behind the farmhouse. As the three hired hands piled into it to go home, Moffat shouted a reminder about something to be picked up from the store on the way to work in the morning.

"If they're going down to the township they could give me a lift," said Celia.

Reacting to a scowl from Watson, Moffat said: "It's thirty-five miles. You're tired and hungry. My wife will take care of you and we'll get you down to the township in the morning."

No, thought Celia. she was frightened of him, even more frightened of the fat and sinister Watson, anxious to get back in contact with Tom MacRae, and above all eager to change her clothes. She protested that Mrs Moffat must not be put to trouble.

"There won't be any trouble," said Watson, making the remark sound sinister.

Moffat bared very white teeth in a frightening smile and put an arm round her shoulders. "Come on in."

"Off you go, boys," said Watson to the hired hands. The utility roared away, leaving Celia no choice.

After a bath her morale was higher. Mrs Moffat, a haunted little woman with a foreign accent which Celia did not recognize, seemed grateful for female company and chatted away happily while she ministered to her needs. But during the meal she was overawed by the men, who ate in silence. Celia brooded on the fact that with Moffat in charge at Derwent Station and Watson at Mount Shelley, which according to Marano was a state-run cattle breeding establishment, they were both government employees.

Near the end of the meal Celia decided that she was tired of being ignored. "Why is Rose Murphy a 'crazy bitch'?" she asked.

Moffat stared. "Who says?"

"You did, when you shouted up to me in the tree."

He shrugged, but said nothing.

"It was losink her husband sent her crazy," said Mrs Moffat, embarrassed by his silence. "That's why she drink too much. Edward, show the lady what she has done to you at the church barbecue."

"No."

"She drink too much, and with a steak knife she made a great cut in my Edward's arm, and—"

Watson blurted out an interruption. "She's crazy, that's all."

Mrs Moffat jumped in her chair and fell silent. Her husband had just kicked her under the table.

"You mean, she attacked you with a knife?" Celia asked him.

"She fell over a bench, it was an accident," said Moffat. "Anyhow, it was only a scratch."

Mrs Moffat began to clear the table and Celia got up to help.

"Leave that, Effie will do the dishes," said Moffat. "Come through here."

It was an order, not an invitation. He and Watson took her into the farm office. There was a desk and two chairs and a filing cabinet. Watson sat down his huge bulk on a corner of the desk, close to Celia. The interrogation was about to begin.

"You were trespassing," said Watson.

"I suppose so, yes."

"You saw the notice on the gate?"

"Yes."

"But you climbed over it. Why?"

"I was following Mrs Murphy. She had stolen some photographs from me and I wanted them back."

"So you say, but when we found you, you were four miles from the Mount Ephraim road, hiding in a tree."

"I was lost, and I'd heard you crashing about in the undergrowth. I thought you were some savage New Zealand animal."

Watson waved this aside as unbelievable and Moffat gave a snort of disgust.

"You're from the UK," Watson snapped. "You met Rosie while she was over there last winter, right?"

"No, wrong. I met her for the first time yesterday."

More scornful noises dismissed this as even less believable.

"I bet she's told you a whole lot of things that are none of your business, eh?"

"About what in particular?"

"About why she's set up this stunt about the dam, about why she's out to have the pants off Trev Thornhill, about why she's snooping around on Mount Ephraim, about why she went to the UK last winter and who she met there—"

"I've only had three short conversations with her, two of them with other people present and none of these subjects came up. I'm sorry to disappoint you."

Watson got up off the desk and stood over her, with his great belly almost in her face. "You *do* disappoint me, dear. We find you trespassing on Mount Ephraim land and you're not frank with us. This story of yours doesn't make sense."

"I haven't told you any story yet. All I've done is to deny the story you've made up and tried to bully me into telling."

"Let's hear the true story then."

"I don't see why. You two are Department of Agriculture employees working on state farms, and nothing to do with Mount Ephraim. What I was doing on Mr Thornhill's property is a matter between him and me and none of your business. And now, if I may, I'd like to use your telephone."

"What for?"

"To tell them at Kirkstone where I am. You don't want this whole mountainside overrun with search parties looking for me in the morning?"

She watched them thinking this out and decided that their position was rather weak. Refusing her the phone would mean admitting that she was being held prisoner and not a mere overnight guest. Watson nodded a grudging approval and Moffat handed her the phone.

She rang Rose Murphy's house. She might not be there, but it was the botanists' headquarters and the simplest way of getting a message to Marano to stop him raising the alarm.

Her ring was answered at once. "Rosie?" asked Marano's tense voice.

"No, it's Celia Grant. I'm sorry if I've been a worry but I got lost in the bush and I'm at Derwent Station. I'll be spending the night here. Would you tell Dr MacRae, who'll be wondering where I've got to? He's staying at the Sunnybank Motel."

Ignoring all this, Marano only replied: "Where's Rosie?"

"Isn't she back yet?"

"No, and when we returned here the house had been broken into and ransacked from top to bottom, all the drawers emptied, everything upside-down. It is all very unsatisfactory and confusing. I insist on knowing what has happened to her."

"I'm afraid I don't know, why ask me?"

"When she was last seen, you were making a brutal attack on her."

Of course. He had witnessed the Murphy-Grant bout of fisticuffs.

"To be accurate," Celia corrected, "she attacked me."

"That is quite untrue, I saw it myself. If anything has happened to her, you will have to answer some awkward questions."

"Dear me, what nonsense you talk," said Celia lightly, and put the phone down.

"News desk, please. This is Lance Johnson in Kirkstone. There's been an important development, I have a new lead to the story I filed last night. Ready? Okay, I'll go ahead. 'Red Rosie has been murdered stop. The body of Rose Murphy comma, firebrand left-wing member of parliament and widow of disgraced Ted Murphy comma, was found shortly before ten this morning by search parties which set out at dawn stop. She was lying deep in the bush on land belonging to the Mount Ephraim sheep station comma, and had been shot at close range in the chest with a twelve-bore shotgun which was lying several yards away stop.' Got that? Now pick up last night's story at the

second sentence where I say the alarm was raised because she failed to keep appointments yesterday afternoon for press and television interviews. Okay, and tell Jeff I'll stay here overnight and phone him about future coverage in the morning. 'Bye."

❧ FIVE ❧

By mid-morning all the search parties had been reassembled and ushered off Mount Ephraim land by Thornhill and Moffat and Watson, who had assumed responsibility for keeping the inquisitive away from the scene of the crime. They made an exception for Dr MacRae, who was seized on when he emerged from the bush and hurried to the spot to give the police an expert medical opinion.

The tough line Celia took with Moffat and Watson had paid off. Though obviously puzzled, they had been much more polite and made what was probably a pretence of accepting her account of her reasons for being found where she was. She had tried to lead the searchers to the place where she had last seen Rosie disappear among the trees, but the maze of tracks made by wild animals confused her and she could give only a rough indication. Hours of searching had followed, but now it was over. The volunteers were standing around outside the Mount Ephraim gate, talking in low voices or getting into their cars to go back to the township. Celia was tired and also, she realized, hungry. The remains of yesterday's picnic were in her anorak pocket, but she hesitated to eat them publicly so soon after the discovery of Rosie's body, lest this seem heartless. So she hid behind some Mahoe* shrubs, faintly surprised to find herself wolfing milk chocolate in the presence of death while taking cover behind the largest member of the violet family known to botany.

Her munching was interrupted by an interesting conversation close behind her between two men, talking in low voices.

"This time they gone too blimin' far."

"Think they did it?"

"Must have."

"Why would they?"

"She went crook at Thornhill at the meeting."

"That's no reason for killing someone."

"What reason was there for the Harrisons' wool-shed? Or them sheep on the Hodson run? Or Sammy Wilson's dog?"

"They all spoke out of turn. Harrison had a few beers in the hotel and talked about what he saw when he worked at Mount Shelley. Sammy let on about how Crampton fiddled things for them. Hodson, I don't know. Same sort of thing, though."

"Murder's different, they never went that far before."

---

*Mahoe (*Melictus ramiflorus*) is a shrub or small tree with white bark, hence its common name of Whitey Wood. The flowers are insignificant, but the purple berries are striking.

"Maybe Rosie knew something. They say her husband did."

"You going to say anything?"

There was a long pause. "Let the police puzzle it out."

"They won't, not if no one tells them anything."

An even longer silence. "We don't *know* it was them, do we?"

"That's right, it could be anyone. I'm not taking any risks."

"Nor me. I don't want my woolshed burnt down."

They moved away. As soon as it seemed safe Celia came out of hiding and tried to identify the speakers, but they had merged with the crowd and she could not be sure. What she had just heard was riveting. It explained why the meeting in the woolshed had been so docile until Bazzer and friends stirred it up, and the wider implications were startling. They would have to be thought about carefully, but her immediate aim was to cadge a lift back to the township. She went over to Marano's minibus and asked if he had room for her.

"Mrs Grant, I want no dealings with you. You were her enemy."

He was eating a ham sandwich. The note of high tragedy would have been more effective if he had not spoken with his mouth full. He gave a huge swallow, and added: "When she was last seen you were making a brutal attack on her. The police will want to know why."

"I've told you, it was the other way round. I'd like to know why she made a brutal attack on me."

"You are lying!" cried Marano. "She was the most generous, the most even-tempered of women, she

82

would never have attacked anyone without provocation. You will have to account for your behaviour to the police."

"Well, no doubt you will give them your version of the quarrel and I shall give mine. I know you're very distressed, Mr Marano, and I can make allowances, but you obviously think I killed Mrs Murphy so we may as well discuss it calmly. If the police ask you what I was carrying, if anything, when I got into the minibus yesterday morning, what will you tell them?"

He looked blank.

"It's an important question," she went on. "According to people who've seen the body, she was killed with a twelve-bore shotgun which was found at the scene of the crime. Everyone who was in that minibus knows that I had no such thing about me at any time during yesterday's expedition, so where did I find a twelve-bore shotgun to kill her with? They don't grow on trees."

A silence fell. Marano examined his half-eaten sandwich sheepishly, but decided against taking another bite. "There is no limit to your enmity," he complained. "Dr MacRae says you have been making absurd suggestions about the plants in the gorge, in a deliberate attempt to besmirch her memory."

"Oh really, when I made them she didn't have a memory to besmirch because she was still alive. Besides, they're not absurd at all. Dr MacRae and I reached the same conclusion independently. Have another look and you'll see that I'm right."

"How can you be right? Where did the plants come from if they're cultivated, answer me that. No respectable specialist grower would co-operate in a deception of that sort. You can prove nothing, and should keep your pernicious ideas to yourself out of respect for her memory."

"I can't be a party to twisting scientific facts."

"They are not facts, the authorities agree that 'many alpine plants have very wide environmental tolerances, allowing them to grow in a range of habitats'. And remember, this discovery has stirred up a lot of interest, we have international opinion behind us now in the fight against the dam. If you start spreading these wild suggestions, ignorant people will be taken in and you will do enormous damage to the whole conservationist movement."

"I don't agree, the sooner the conservationist movement is prevented from making itself ridiculous, the less the damage will be."

He gaped at her like an alarmed fish. He was in a panic, she realized. Excited by his discoveries and anxious to please a beautiful celebrity who had unexpectedly admitted him to her bed, he had suppressed any doubts he felt and overlooked things he should have noticed. But now that his mistake had been pointed out, he knew he had touched off a major conservationist agitation on the basis of highly suspicious data. If his findings came under serious attack his academic reputation, such as it was, would be in ruins.

"One can always be mistaken," he stammered. "I . . . may have judged your attitude to Mrs Murphy too harshly. Equally, I think you should weigh the botanical evidence more carefully before you jump to conclusions. One must always be prepared to compromise."

It was an interesting suggestion: if she kept her botanical doubts to herself, he would make his account of her quarrel with Rosie a little less lurid when he gave it to the police. Such ideas must, however, be stamped on firmly.

"Oh no," said Celia easily, "it's never wise to fudge the facts when the police are involved. And I'm sorry, but scientific fraud can't be hushed up simply because someone's dead. Let's both tell the truth as we see it and keep things simple."

Marano glared. "You hated her. You are determined to blacken her memory, and you will suffer for it, I shall see to that. I owe it to her. I was her lover, you see."

"Brrr. This place is an ice house, Parsons. And draughty."

"Alpine houses is always kept cold, Your Grace, with the windows open. Them things like it cold, being accustomed to surviving on the bare mountain tops in bitter weather. You could grow them in the open, except that they need protecting from the wet."

"Now where are the New Zealand alpines that His Lordship's so proud of?"

"Here, Your Grace. All along the bench on this side."

"What miserable little affairs. Hardly worth bothering with."

"Yes, Your Grace. I dunno what His Lordship sees in them. I like a nice calceolaria myself."

"I wonder, Parsons, if you remember the red-headed New Zealand lady who was staying in the village last summer?"

"Wee hee hee hee! Woo ha ha ha! She was a one, Your Grace."

"Quite. She came up here several times while His Lordship was pottering about in the greenhouses. I thought perhaps you might remember."

"Hee hee hee. She was a one all right."

"I wonder why she came. Was she specially interested in New Zealand alpines?"

"Not her. Pretended to be, but she couldn't tell a raoulia from a Brussels sprout. She was after His Lordship, woo ha ha ha!"

"I quite agree with you Parsons, 'woo ha ha ha' is a very apt comment. What would a raving beauty like that want with an old wreck like His Lordship? Money?"

"I dunno, Your Grace. All I know is, she wanted something from him and he wouldn't give it to her."

"Really? How d'you know? . . . Come on, don't be shy. I eavesdrop a lot myself when it's necessary."

"I was in the orchid house, see? Well, His Lordship calls it the orchid house, but there's tomatoes and all sorts in there nowadays, and I was watering the tommies down at the far end, and they come in. She was chasing him like, and the gangways between the staging's narrow in there and she got right up against him in her thin dress and nothing underneath it and her bosoms all wobbly, woo ha ha ha, and she was saying there must be a way, you can think of one if you try, and he kept saying no no me dear, out of the question, quite impractical."

"But you don't know what was out of the question?"

"No, Your Grace, because me watering can made a

gurgle like they do sometimes when they're nearly empty, and she noticed me and dragged His Lordship out of the greenhouse and they went on arguing about it outside. But I reckon she didn't get no satisfaction out of His Lordship, because she took herself off soon after looking as cross as an owl with toothache.''

"How odd. I suppose he went round later to the bed-and-breakfast place where she was staying and made it up.''

"No, Your Grace. That was the last anyone saw of her. She sent for Tibbins's taxi and made him take her to the afternoon train. His Lordship was that put out when he found she'd gone.''

Celia hitched an uncomfortable lift back to the township in the open load space of a farmer's utility. Her first concern was to find a telephone. As the last person to have seen Rose Murphy alive she could hardly leave Kirkstone until she had been interviewed by the police, and Lucy must be warned not to expect her back in Wellington on the evening plane. There was a phone box in the main street, but it was besieged by reporters who had appeared from nowhere like vultures at the scent of death. A corner of Crampton's general store proved to house a sub-post office and a telephone with a slightly shorter queue. After waiting for some time among galvanized buckets and rolls of wire she took her turn in the booth and rang the airline in Christchurch to cancel her flight, then dialled Lucy's number in Wellington.

"Hullo love, it's Mum," she began. "Did I wake you?"

"Yes, thank goodness. I was dreaming that I'd given birth to a very bad-tempered rattlesnake."

"How nasty dear, you should read something pure by Barbara Cartland to stop you being morbid. Listen, I'm stuck here till I've been seen by the police, because guess who has been most inconveniently murdered."

"I know, it was on the midday news. Did you get any sense out of her before that happened?"

"No. Only a few words of complete nonsense."

"Pity. Your Duchess rang, sounding very distraught and asking what you'd found out. She says will you ring her as soon as possible."

"Very well, but not now, it's three in the morning there. Is she at Melsingham?"

"She didn't say. D'you know who shot Red Rosie?"

"No."

"I bet it was one of her lovers. Jim's been asking around, she seems to have had them in droves."

"That reminds me, could you ask Jim to do something for me? I've been thinking, she was an MP, so she must have a secretary. Could he try to locate her for me? She may be able to tell us what went on besides sex between Bertie and her employer."

"Right. Will do. Anything else?"

"No, I must go now, there are people waiting to use the phone. I hate being stuck here with the baby coming, hang on to it tight till I can get away."

She stepped out of the booth and found herself besieged by the media. Was she Mrs Grant? Was it true that she had quarrelled with Mrs Murphy shortly before her death? What about? Was it a real fight, and if so who won? She smiled graciously but said nothing, and managed by dodging among the buckets and rolls of wire to walk out of the shop. A tourist coach had just arrived and the passengers, mostly old age pensioners, were forming two cheerful queues outside the public lavatory. She joined the female one and went on saying nothing and smiling at the media from her place in a row of solidly built women until the media withdrew, baffled.

Back in the camper her thoughts were disagreeable. To judge from the media's questions, Marano had made the Grant-Murphy fight sound like an event worthy of Madison Square Gardens, and done a thorough job of publicizing it, all of which would do her no good with the police when they questioned her. As an antidote to gloom she switched on the radio, and was even more depressed to hear a botanical pundit explain that the discoveries in the Kirkstone Valley had shattered all preconceived ideas about the history of plant life in the South Island during glacial times. Hitherto it had been thought that Fiordland and Nelson (in the extreme north and south) were the only significant refuges for alpine plants during a period when the intervening area was severely glaciated, but now . . . She switched the radio off. Someone was banging violently on the door of the camper.

"Who's there. I'm not talking to the press," she called.

An angry face appeared at one window after another: Marano's. He was leaping about outside like an agitated dog. Celia let down the driver's window to parley with him.

"I must ask you to remove this vehicle from Mrs

Murphy's property at once," he snarled. "You have no right to be here."

"Are you in charge now?" she asked.

"I have assumed responsibility until her legal representatives arrive."

"Oh well done. Who are they?"

"I have no idea and it is no concern of yours. Do you intend to move away or not?"

"I suppose so, if you're going to behave like Ivan the Terrible till I do."

"The house has been ransacked once already. Someone has to guard it."

"How extraordinary about the burglary. What was stolen?"

"We don't know, and the only person who could tell us has been brutally murdered. It is all most unsatisfactory, like your part in this affair."

"It could have been teenagers. They always make a lot of mess."

"I think not. Small sums of money have been left untouched."

"How about Bazzer and Co? As a revenge for being thrown out of the party?"

Where were they, she wondered suddenly. They had not been in evidence during the search for Rosie, and there was no sign of them in the township. Jessie was very strong-minded; perhaps she had marched them away long ago to storm more worthwhile political strongholds in the north.

Marano awoke to the fact that he was gossiping about the burglary with his loved one's arch enemy, and told her haughtily that these were matters he would discuss at the proper time with the police. As that seemed to be that, Celia drove the camper out into the street and left it there while she enquired for an alternative site. But where to ask? The door of Brown's Hotel stood invitingly open, but it was full of male beer-drinkers, all standing up, and was obviously no place for a lady in search of information. She tried the store instead. There was a woman behind the counter with dyed black hair, who stared at her with black boot-button eyes for a long time before answering her query.

"I'll fetch Mr Crampton," she said and withdrew into the back premises. After conversing with someone in an undertone she reappeared with Mr Crampton, a hollow-cheeked man with yellowish whites to his eyes. "You Mrs Grant?" he asked.

Celia agreed that she was.

"Came here for the meeting, did you?"

It was a regular interrogation, covering the route by which Celia had arrived in Kirkstone as well as her impressions of New Zealand and of Kirkstone in particular. She was beginning to wonder if her query about a site for her camper would ever be answered when Mr Crampton said abruptly: "Behind the motel. There's a toilet and a shower there that you can use. Two dollars a night. Show her, Emmy."

The area behind the motel proved to be a small camping site, empty except for a disused-looking trailer caravan in one corner. Celia wondered why her credentials had been gone into so thoroughly before she was allowed to use it.

Walking back through the motel to the street to fetch the camper, she said: "How dreadful that there have been two tragic deaths in that family now, her husband's and now hers. And that poor young girl who was mixed up in it, I believe she came from a local household?''

The black boot-button eyes stared at her. "What business is that of yours?"

It was an embarrassingly crude way of extracting information, but Celia was satisfied with the results. If the girl had not been local, it would have been natural to tell a nosy-parker so.

She had just settled the camper into the site and was thinking of making contact with Tom MacRae when a police constable presented himself: would she please come with him to the schoolhouse, where Inspector Brent would like a word with her?

She complied, but was grateful for the police escort as they crossed the yard of the motel, which the journalists seemed to have adopted as their headquarters. In reply to their hopeful enquiries whether she was under arrest she replied cheerfully, "Not that I know of," and passed on. At the schoolhouse the policeman made her wait in a kind of lobby with pegs for the children's coats and hats. A murmur of men's voices came from the schoolroom. After a time the door opened and Harry Watson, the gloomy faced manager of the Mount Shelley cattle breeding station, came out. He was followed by a blond young police officer in crisply laundered shirtsleeves.

"Thank you, Mr Watson, that's very important information," he said. "I'll follow it up at once."

Watson threw Celia a self-important nod, as if to say: "There, you see, I am a power in the land, the police listen to me—so watch out."

When he had gone the blond police officer treated

Celia to a bright smile which symbolized efficiency rather than warmth of welcome. "You'll be Mrs Grant, is that right? I'm Inspector Brent, would you come in please?"

He sat her down on a rickety bentwood chair and installed himself behind the teacher's desk. He was a pleasant-looking young man, but his expression made it rather too clear that he was delighted with his looks and the muscles bulging under his shirt and his promotion to inspector at an unusually early age.

"You're from the UK," he said.

Was it imagination, or had the "UK" been said with a faint undertone of distaste?

He dealt rapidly with the preliminaries of name, address, length of stay in New Zealand, and the fact that she seemed to be the last person to have seen Rosie alive. "And you came to Kirkstone to attend the meeting and her press conference afterwards."

"No, not exactly. I wanted some information from her." She explained about Bertie's disappearance, his family's need to contact him over a business matter, and the photographs which linked him with Rose Murphy. Watching him as she spoke, she decided that she was right about the reaction of distaste, it reappeared even more markedly at the mention of Bertie's rank; being a pommie lord was even worse than being a pommie woman. Some earlier visitor from Britain must have given him grave offence.

She took out one of the photos of Bertie that Hermione had given her and put it on the desk. "You may find that useful for identification, if he turns out to be connected with the case."

"Why should he be?"

"He has been here recently and taken photos not only of Rose Murphy, but also of the plants whose discovery caused such a sensation yesterday."

"You'll have to show me these photos."

"I can't. Mrs Murphy denied all knowledge of Lord Albert and snatched them from me. There was a struggle, and it was after that that I followed her up the Mount Ephraim road and into the bush."

Inspector Brent nodded, as if he knew all about the fight already and did not attach much importance to her account of it. "Now can we be a bit more detailed about this, Mrs Grant. There was a ute parked outside the locked gate over the cattle stop, did you go anywhere near it?"

"I'm sorry. A what?"

"A ute," he repeated, putting on an act of fury at her stupidity. "It was parked outside the gate, next to Mrs Murphy's trail bike."

"Would you please explain the meaning of the word 'ute'?"

He spoke loudly and slowly, as if to a deaf idiot. "A ute is a farmer's utility vehicle with seats for three persons in front and a load space behind, don't you have them in the UK?"

Celia decided that some haughty Englishwoman must have inflicted a king-size wound on his sexual pride, nothing less could account for such behaviour. But what was all this about a parked vehicle?

"I don't understand, there must be some mistake," she said. "There was no utility parked outside that gate when I climbed over it."

"He signed impatiently. "Let me get this straight. You're *denying* that you saw it?"

"I most certainly am. Whoever says it was there must have got their timing wrong."

"You ought to think again about this, Mrs Grant. Two of Mr Moffat's men from Derwent Station were repairing the fence near where it crosses the river, a fallen tree had busted it down. They parked the ute up by the gate and went down to the river on foot."

"Either they've got their timing wrong or they're talking about a different gate."

Brent paused impressively. "Mrs Grant, if you're taking this line I think you should have legal advice."

"Oh, I don't think that's necessary, Inspector. I have nothing to hide." She forced a smile. I mustn't show how much I dislike him, she thought, with his self-satisfied good looks and his bullying manner. I must try not to sound like an upper-class British lady despising the colonials, he probably has some good reason for disliking poms. . . .

Brent shrugged, as if to say that not having a lawyer was her funeral, not his. "Let's go back to this story of yours about some photographs that you say Mrs Murphy snatched from you. Why would she want to do that?"

"It was understandable. Some of them were of herself in the nude—"

"What? Oh no, Mrs Grant."

"I know it sounds incredible, but it was so. There were also some studies of the rare plants, and it was obvious from the circumstances that they were photographed before their alleged discovery. In other words, they proved that the plants were fakes."

"Expert opinion doesn't agree with you about that."

"Tom MacRae says I'm right. Marano insists that they're genuine, if you call him an expert. Anyway, Mrs Murphy was very angry when I showed her the pictures. After a lot of bluster she said they'd been stolen from her and she wanted them back."

"Stolen, were they? How did they got into your possession?"

He fiddled impatiently with a pencil while she explained about the letter rack at Bertie's club.

"But if they were stolen—" he began.

"She *said* they were stolen. It may not have been true."

"Why did you refuse to give them to her?"

"I didn't have time to refuse, she snatched them away too quickly. I think the point was, she didn't want to answer questions about them."

"And you say you followed her to get them back."

"What I really wanted was some sensible answers to a few simple questions."

Brent drummed with his fingers on the desk, then stood up.

"I'm not satisfied with your story, Mrs Grant. I shall want to question you again. Don't leave Kirkstone till I tell you you may."

"But I must get back to Wellington. My daughter's expecting her first baby there early next week."

"You could speed things up by giving me some truthful answers for a change. There are two things wrong with your story: Rose Murphy was far too experienced a politician to let herself be photographed naked, and secondly, no photos of any kind were found on or near her body. That will be all for the moment, Mrs Grant."

Shaken by this encounter, she started back to the camper. To her relief there were no journalists about in the forecourt of the motel, so she looked in at the windows of the units as she passed, trying to identify Tom MacRae's. When she found the right one he saw her too and invited her in.

"How did it go with Brent?" he asked. "Nasty feller, throws his weight around."

"We didn't take to each other and he seems to believe I killed Mrs Murphy, but I can't think why. I didn't have a shotgun, everyone who was in the minibus knows that. How could I have killed her?"

"The gun was lying on the driver's seat of the utility."

"Wait. I still don't understand. What is this about a utility?"

"The gun was in the utility that was parked outside the gate on the road to Mount Ephraim."

"No Tom, there was nothing parked there. Who says there was?"

"Two men of Moffat's. He sent them up from Derwent Station to mend a gap in the fence. One of them had a gun, hoping for a wild turkey or something for the pot. The break in the fence was down by the river and there was a lot to carry, tools and wire and what not. Left the gun in the cab of the utility, he said, and when he came back, no gun."

"Horrors," said Celia when this had sunk in. "It makes sense, doesn't it? I run after Rosie and I see a gun and I'm beside myself with rage after our quarrel, so I seize the gun and slaughter her with it. Except that there was no utility there and consequently no gun. Honestly Tom, someone made this whole story up."

There was a shocked silence. What would he say, Celia wondered, if she asked him whether he believed her? To stave off the moment of truth she went on talking. "This is all rather awkward. That policeman has a hang-up about people from Britain, Derwent and Shelley have decided I'm up to no good, and Marano hates my guts for saying his rarities are fakes and slandering the Blessed and Venerable Rose Murphy. I shall be burnt at the stake if I'm not arrested first for murder."

What happened next was even more awkward. MacRae seized both her hands. His bright blue eyes bored into her. He had already mentioned rather too casually that he was a widower.

"I belive you, Celia," he said. "If you say the utility wasn't there, then it wasn't. Let me help you, I can handle Brent."

She drew her hands away. "Oh, I refuse to quake with terror, the whole thing's too ridiculous. I can't take it seriously."

"You should, Celia. This place has a nasty feel, there was a spooky atmosphere at that meeting, people are afraid to talk."

Celia was reminded of what she had overheard behind the Mahoe bushes up at the Mount Ephraim gate. "The point is that 'they' punish you if you speak out of turn. Someone called Harrison had his wool-shed burnt down. Two other people had trouble, one of them over some sheep and the other with something nasty happening to a dog."

"Who's 'they'?" MacRae asked.

"Derwent and Mount Shelley for a start. And

Crampton, the hatchet-faced man who owns the store and this motel. Unless I misheard he fiddles things for 'them'.''

"Is Thornhill in it too?"

"Probably."

"But what is the 'it' that they're all in? Some fiendish plan for world domination in alliance with the Japs?"

"Celia, you must take this seriously," he insisted. "They've a secret to keep and a murder means policemen asking questions that they won't want to answer. They need a scapegoat from outside, and they've picked on you. The township is all tensed up already. I read a play once by Arthur Miller—"

"*The Crucible*? About the witches of Salem? And me as a scapegoat in a crucible, like a missionary in a pot?"

"Don't joke about this, Celia. You have no idea how hysterical small isolated communities can get."

"Very well, I'll be serious. She couldn't have shot herself?"

"No. The gun was too far away and it had been wiped clean of fingerprints. Willie Brent's bone from the neck up. He got his promotion for sheer brutality, sorting out a hydro-electric company town where there was a lot of crime. He won't find out who killed her, we must."

"Fine, but where do we start among all these loose ends? What was Rosie doing, rushing off like that into the bush? Where on earth did all those plants come from? Where does Bertie fit in and who is the fat man with the beard in the photograph?"

"Whoa, Celia, whoa! Who's Bertie? What photograph?"

By the time she had filled him in on these questions, their mental confusion was worse than ever.

"We have to start somewhere," said Celia, "so why not with the fact that yesterday while everyone was gaping at the alleged rarities in the gorge, Rosie's house was broken into and ransacked. We know, don't we, what the burglar was looking for."

MacRae gave a warning twinkle. "Extraordinary spectacle, that."

"Sorry. Too difficult. Explain."

"At the meeting. Othello and Desdemona snatching the hankie from each other."

"That's right, Tom. Othello looking appalled because Desdemona had got it, and Desdemona looking as if something she hadn't the faintest suspicion of had just dawned on her."

He nodded. "She saw why he didn't want her to have it, eh? So of course he had to get it back and burgled her house. Didn't find it though."

"How d'you know?"

"The house was ransacked from top to bottom, only thieves looking everywhere for anything worth having do that. If you're after something definite you stop looking when you find it."

"Unless it's too well hidden for you to find," said Celia. "Or—wait, she could have put it in the post, before she left on the trail bike to go up the gorge. We could ask at the post office."

"No. It's a sub-agency at the store and Crampton's one of 'them'. He'd report it at once if we asked. I'll check with Christchurch. If she sent it there I know where it will be."

"Why Christchurch?" she objected.

"Why would she go further afield?"

"Would they tell you?"

"Yes, I know them from when I was in practice. Go and phone, will we? Before they shut up shop for the night?"

"D'you mind if I stay here? The media will be on the prowl."

He clapped on the battered felt hat and opened the door.

"She may have sent samples there before," Celia called after him. "Do ask them."

While he was gone she worried about him. He was a good ally with useful connections, but exploiting him while preventing the emotional volcano from erupting would be tricky and perhaps not very ethical. . . . Giving up the problem, she looked at the books on his bedside table. *Ways of Escape* by Graham Greene, Marina Warner on the cult of the Virgin Mary. Bought copies, not from a library.

Before she could dip far into either he came back, grinning broadly from under the hat. "We struck lucky," he reported. "They got it this morning and ran the tests at once. Thornhill is blood group 'O'. Your hunch was right too. Rosie sent them two other samples earlier."

"When exactly?"

"One ten days ago, that was an 'AB' rhesus negative. Another a fortnight earlier, a group 'A'. No names. Sample one and sample two."

"Splendid, in that case there's something I want to check. Where are the media?"

"In the hotel, pumping beer into themselves and misinformation out of the locals."

"Come along then, I'll risk it. But bring a flash-lamp."

Giving the open door of the hotel a wide berth, she led him into the porch of the little white-painted church and used the flashlamp to scan the notices about Sunday services and jumble sales. "Ah, here we are, people never bother to take it down when the thing's over. The 'AB' rhesus negative is Moffat."

He looked at the notice. "It doesn't say that. What it says is, the Churchwomen's Guild barbecue will take place a fortnight ago tomorrow."

"Quite. Moffat was at the barbecue and so was Rosie, pretending to be rather drunk. She staged an 'accident' with a steak knife and make a long scratch on his arm. Two days later the sample turned up in the path lab at Christchurch."

"Ah. Lots to think about there. You getting hungry? I am."

On thinking it over Celia found that she was ready for the early evening meal which New Zealanders call "tea".

"I have tins in my camper. Unless you prefer the tourists' café."

He took her elbow gently and steered her back towards the motel. "I have steak for two."

Having poured her a powerful scotch and water, he began cooking competently and without fuss. "Now. If the 'AB' rhesus negative ten days ago is Moffat, who's the group 'A' a fortnight before that?"

"The baby. Or its mother," said Celia. "Either way the thing begins to make sense. Rosie was collecting blood samples, to prove that her husband wasn't the father. She suspected that Moffat was and I see why. He's very dark and hairy, I'd say the local all-purpose Heathcliff to look at him, but she was wrong. The child was Thornhill's."

"Ah," said MacRae, making gravy.

"Thornhill must have realized what she was up to. Perhaps he was at the barbecue, or he may have known about her knifing the baby or its mother for the earlier group 'A' sample. When he sees that he's bled into her hankie he panics and gives himself away."

The warning twinkle appeared in MacRae's eye. "She saw he'd panicked. He saw she saw he'd panicked. So he panicked again, because he spotted that she'd spotted why he panicked the first time."

"Or to simplify the thing a little," said Celia, "he knew he'd admitted to Rosie that he was the real father of the baby that was palmed off on Ted Murphy."

"Yes. Next question. If Thornhill's the father, why did Ted Murphy shoot himself?"

"Easy, Tom. The girl's a nymphet with the morals of a Port Said alley cat, must have been or why would she have anything to do with a whiskery old fatty like Thornhill? When she gets pregnant he tells her to set a honey-trap for Murphy, who falls for it and believes her when she says he's the father."

"Yes, good. Why pick on Murphy though? Anyone would do."

"I see what you mean," said Celia. "You think Murphy was sniffing around at this awful secret that no one must know. So Thornhill sets him up for a character assassination before he can do any harm.''

''Right. And now the fat's in the fire. Rosie knows what he's done.''

''And for all he knows she can prove it, unless he gets the blood sample back before she can have it analysed. He searches her house and can't find it, so—''

''That's right, he kills her,'' said MacRae, dishing steak out on to plates. ''Here you are, let's eat.''

✿ SIX ✿

"Now Celia, have you found Bertie?" asked Hermione from the other side of the world.

"No. And before I could get any sense out of Rose Murphy she was murdered."

"How typical, she would be. I mean how deeply tragic and at the same time inconvenient, but never mind that, Celia dear, I've lots to tell you so listen carefully. According to Bertie's disgusting gardener the Murphy woman wanted Bertie to do something for her and when he said he couldn't, it wasn't practical, she was furious and walked out on him. The filthy old creature can't even eavesdrop efficiently, he doesn't know what she wanted Bertie to do—"

"I can guess. She hoped he'd give her a lot of his celmisias and things from his alpine house so that she could pass them off as wild plants, but it couldn't be done because they'd flowered already in the northern hemisphere."

"I don't understand a word you're saying, Celia dear, but never mind, listen to this. After she'd gone Bertie was in a foul temper for days, because of course there was no bed of roses with Rosie anymore. Then on October the twenty-third someone called Sir Edward Bolton died, or rather he did it in Australia a bit earlier, and on October the twenty-third he was in *The Times*, and Muriel says Bertie got very excited when he saw the obit and shot away like one of those Cape Canaveral things the very same day."

"Where to? To join up with Rosie?"

"Everard thinks not, he went to the forwarding address she gave her landlady and it was a bank. She must have decided to ditch Bertie when he couldn't do whatever it was she wanted."

"Has Everard found out when Bertie left England?"

"No dear, only that he was issued a new passport on November the twelfth, so he must have been here then. But Everard says he didn't appear at his club or his hairdresser's, or any of his usual places, so what he was doing around then is a mystery."

"What address did the Foreign Office send his new passport to?"

"Maddeningly, they won't say. This is a private matter between them and Bertie and God."

Celia collected her thoughts. "Now about . . . Sir Edward Bolton, did you say? What did Bertie find so exciting about him?"

"Goodness knows dear, a very dim career according to *Who's Who*, Northern Nigeria and Aden and all sorts of dreadful places. He was Colonial Office and didn't even make it to Hong Kong, which

I'm told is quite amusing. And when we stopped having colonies they took pity on all those people and let them into the Foreign Office, and he just managed to scrape up a knighthood before they retired him. He was head of mission in Wellington for his last three years."

"Ah. Recently?"

"Ages ago dear, he was eighty."

"Then the tie-up with Bertie can't have happened here. What can it be?"

"Goodness knows, but there must be one. The piece in *The Times* was quite short and Bertie seems to have written one of those extra bits that they publish afterwards, recalling something about the person that wasn't in the official obit. The maddening thing is, he didn't read it out to Muriel so that she could say how clever dear, it isn't that sort of marriage. And *The Times* didn't publish it and threw it away, so we don't know what was in it."

"Did you say Bolton died in Australia?" Celia asked.

"Peacefully at his home in Sydney, according to *The Times*. He must have settled there when he retired. There's an address in *Who's Who*, Fifteen Ocean Drive, Newport Beach, Sydney. Everard says it's one of those stockbrokerish seafront suburbs with huge garages full of boats. You'd better pop over there and investigate."

"Not possibly."

"Why not, Celia? Australia's only next door and we're desperate, we must find Bertie. Why can't you?"

"Apart from geographical considerations, murder suspects are supposed to stay put till they're cleared."

"Murder suspects? What is all this? Who?"

"Me, Hermione. I was the last person to see Rose Murphy alive."

"Nonsense dear, you wouldn't hurt a fly, you're much too small. Ask them for a day off from being suspected and see what you can find out in Sydney."

"Auckland to Sydney is five and half hours by air. I'll have to organize someone else to go, but don't worry, I'll fix something."

"Oh really, Celia. You might as well say 'don't worry' to Juliet when she wakes up in her tomb and finds the stage littered with dead gentlemen."

"What I meant was, I think I can guess why Bertie was so excited when he saw that obit. If I'm right it's the best lead we've had yet, and I'll follow it up somehow."

After a lot more grumbling from Hermione Celia got her off the line and thanked the elderly couple who had allowed her to use their phone and to reverse the charges. Lingering for a gossip, she made another attempt to find out who the girl was in the Ted Murphy sex scandal, but the subject seemed to be strictly taboo. She left hastily by the back when a journalist intent on borrowing the phone presented himself at the front door, and went back to the motel to share Hermione's news with MacRae.

"Bolton," he echoed. "There *is* a Sir somebody Bolton."

"Was," she corrected. "Sir Edward. A botanist? Specializing in alpines? You knew him?"

"Only by name. He was always cropping up, corresponding member of this and that, contributions to the proceedings of learned societies, that sort of thing."

"With a greenhouse?"

He thought for a moment. "Yes. I remember articles illustrated with photos of things he'd grown."

"Then that's why Bertie was so excited. I can't go to Sydney and follow it up, Brent would drag me back here in handcuffs, so why don't you? Hermione would pay your fare."

He looked startled, and began to go pink. "No, Celia, no. I'd worry about you all the time, Brent's a fool and this township is full of knaves. My place is here."

His hands came forward towards her. Celia put hers firmly behind her back, cursing her fatal talent for arousing the protective instincts of men.

"Nonsense, Tom, I'm much tougher than I look. I can take care of myself."

But he had dug his toes in, there was no point in arguing. Who, then, was to go to Sydney? "Where are the journalists?" she asked, suddenly inspired.

"Eating sandwiches in the tourists' café."

"Why don't we let one of them in on it? We could get all the leg-work done for us, it's only a matter of choosing the right newspaper, one with a competent correspondent in Sydney. What's that in your rubbish bin?"

"The paper the steak was wrapped in."

She pulled it out and discovered, legible despite the meat juice, a sensible report from its man in Sydney of a debate in the New South Wales legislature.

"He'll do," she decided. "But have they got a reporter here?"

"Probably, the *Post*'s a Christchurch paper. Want me to find out?"

"Lance Johnson here, is the editor in? . . . Good, put me through. . . . Jeff? I've got an exclusive on the Kirkstone murder. Those rare plants of Rosie's in the ecology story we ran this morning are a fake, grown in greenhouses or gardens, not wild at all."

"Who says?"

"A botanist from the UK called Celia Grant."

"Hell, Lance, I don't like it, she could be crazy."

"I don't think so. Old Dr MacRae, remember him, used to have a practice up Timaru way? He's a very respected botanist on the side and he says she's right."

"I still don't like it. The Australian papers picked up that ecology story from the agencies and made a big play with it, it's been big on radio and television too, everyone's giving the government hell for wanting to drown the pretty flowers. You want me to put all that outcry into reverse on this UK lady's say so?"

"She'll be news herself in a day or two. The police have lined her up as chief murder suspect."

"You mean, we run it as 'murderess slanders her victim, says Rosie's ecology campaign was a fake'?"

"No, we harden up the story before we run it, she's given me a lead for Fred Williams to follow up in Sydney."

"What sort of a lead?"

"There's an old gentleman died in October, lived out at Newport Beach, name of Sir Edward Bolton. MacRae says he used to grow New Zealand alpine plants and write about them in learned journals. Get

110

Ted to find out what happened to them when he died. Did anyone buy them or raid his garden or anything like that, and if so what was taken away and who by? If the same kinds are missing that turned up in the Kirkstone Valley, the story's hard enough to run.''

"Okay, I'll buy it on that basis.''

"Good. One more thing. Do we know the name of the nymphet who figured in the Murphy sex scandal? She's local, but everyone's very tight-lipped about her.''

"I think there was a ruling to withhold her name because she was a minor. Why d'you want to know?''

"The UK botanical lady asked me to find out.''

"Why the hell should we, you got tickets on her? I bet you have, Lance, is she a blonde with boobs like balloons?''

"She is a silver-haired lady about two feet tall who looks like some kind of helpless doll, but she's in possession of all her faculties and then some. She's given us one exclusive and she knows a lot more than she's told us yet. It's in the paper's interests to do her a favour.''

"Okay, we'll see what we can do, but why does she want us to? Did she shoot Red Rosie?''

"If she did she's clever enough to get away with it. Tell Ted to follow up that Sydney lead soonest, will you? We'll have busloads of real heavyweight botanists up here soon to look at Marano's wonder-find, and if they all start shouting that it's a phoney we'll lose the exclusivity.''

"Who's there?'' asked Celia as someone knocked on the door of the camper.

"Inspector Brent. I have some more questions to put to you."

"Oh very well. I'll come across to the schoolhouse in a minute."

"Why don't we talk here?"

"If that's what you want. Come on in."

He climbed into the camper, very aware of himself as a lusty young man invading a woman's quarters. Celia decided that there was no point in trying to appease him, if he had made up his mind that all Englishwomen were haughty bitches, there was nothing she could do about it. She would make mincemeat of him at once.

He sat down opposite her with his chest out and his stomach held in coquettishly, every inch the macho male.

"Do relax, there's no need to be nervous," she said.

His face came to a standstill in mid-smile. "I'm not nervous, Mrs Grant."

"Oh? It looked as if you were holding your breath, but never mind, what did you want to ask me?"

"You claim that Lord Albert Melton visited Mrs Murphy recently here in Kirkstone. No one of that name has been in the township, and I've shown this photo of him around that you gave me. No one recognizes it."

"I see. What is your question?"

"How do you account for the fact that your allegation has proved unfounded?"

"It wasn't an allegation, it was a possibility I had to look into."

Inspector Brent paused impressively and leant

forward. "I put it to you, Mrs Grant, that you invented this whole story. You came here in pursuit of your former lover, Stanley Parker, who had transferred his affections to Mrs Murphy. Your quarrel with her was about Parker, and you shot her in a fit of jealous rage in the vain hope of reclaiming your lover from her."

Celia gaped at him in unaffected amazement. "Would you mind saying all that again?"

He repeated his accusation. His eyes were bulging like urgent blue poached eggs, a sight which made her collapse in helpless laughter.

"Stop that silly noise," squeaked Brent, going falsetto with anger.

Too late, she remembered from previous experience that it was dangerous to laugh at the police. "I'm sorry, but this is absurd. Who on earth is Stanley Parker?"

"You know perfectly well, Mrs Grant."

"I'm sorry, no. And what makes you think I have a lover?"

He looked her over, as one professional beauty inspecting another. "Why not, you're still in quite good shape."

"Please don't be impertinent or I shall have to make an official complaint."

"Why deny it? Your quarrel with Parker at Christchurch airport, when you pleaded with him to return to you, was overheard by a witness."

Celia digested this with difficulty. "Who has been telling you all this nonsense?" she asked. "The same 'witness' who says there was a gun in the utility that wasn't there?"

"No. A hired hand from Mount Shelley who was

delivering a batch of bull semen for air freighting to Napier."

"But I didn't speak to anyone at Christchurch Airport. I got straight into a taxi and did the round of car hire firms, trying to hire something to drive up here in."

"You hired the camper because your appeal to Parker had failed, and drove here to confront him and Mrs Murphy."

Celia decided to take pity on him. "I'm sure we can sort out this muddle you've got yourself into if we discuss it calmly. Tell me about this man Parker."

"I'm here to ask questions, Mrs Grant, not to answer them."

"In that case I can't help you about Parker, so you'd better ask me about something else."

There was a silent battle of wills, which Brent lost. "Parker," he said at length, "has been seen off and on at Mrs Murphy's house all spring, and is obviously her lover."

"What else d'you know about him? Nationality?"

Not even that, it seemed, though he was presumed to be a New Zealander. He had been seen carrying binoculars, presumably for bird-watching as he had enquired about alleged sightings in the area of black stilts.

"They're rare, some say extinct," Brent explained. "They've not been seen around here in living memory, and everyone thought him a bit of a joke."

"What does he look like?" Celia asked.

"Tall and very stout, with a beard."

"Oh, is the beard gray near the roots and darker near the bottom end?"

"Ha!" said Inspector Brent.

"What d'you mean 'Ha'?"

"You've admitted that you know him."

"No, I've admitted that I recognize the description. He's on the reel of film that I mentioned to you this morning. There's a full-length photo of him on it, standing on the porch of Mrs Murphy's house."

"Taken after he transferred his affections from you to her."

"Oh, do use your common sense," she cried, losing patience. "If I wanted a lover, would a woman of my size and build saddle herself with a six-foot-high mountain of fat like Parker? No, don't say anything, it was probably going to be coarse and I don't want to hear it."

"Parker was seen in the township late that evening—"

"Which evening?"

"The one before the meeting in the wool shed. He was asking in an agitated manner for Mrs Murphy, and *he has not been seen since*."

"I expect he went to bed with her in an agitated manner and left early in the morning to avoid causing gossip."

"This is no joking matter. His disappearance has not been accounted for."

"How sinister, but don't look at me. I was still haggling with car hire firms in Christchurch and didn't get here till the afternoon of the next day."

Brent looked at her with baffled loathing. "You still deny your association with him?"

"Yes. Have you any more questions?"

"Not for the present."

"Well, this is your last chance. As I told you, my daughter's expecting her first baby and I really must get back to Wellington. You can ring me there, or if necessary I can come back."

"Let me have a medical certificate. Then I'll consider whether you can be allowed to leave."

"How kind. Would you also consider why certain people are arranging for you to put all the wrong questions to me instead of asking them the right ones? Unless you do, you'll make a fool of yourself over this case."

It was early morning. Tom MacRae's car was old but comfortable and soared up the steep road through the gorge in fine style. He parked it inconspicuously a few hundred yards below the Mount Ephraim gate and Celia got out, shivering a little. The high snow alps loomed from time to time through holes in drifting mist. Plants she had never seen before beckoned from the roadside. I must not dawdle and botanize, she told herself, we have business to do.

The Mount Ephraim gate was no longer padlocked. Inside it the road curved between dark trees and verges powdered with dust from the dirt surface. This was where Celia had had her last glimpse of Rosie and the problem to be solved was, where had she been going in such a hurry? Further, perhaps, than one would normally plan to walk. She had intended to go all the way on the trail bike, but the padlocked gate had forced her to take to her legs instead.

Just round the bend Celia paused. "This is where she turned off into the bush."

MacRae nodded and started off down the narrow

track which branched off the road. It was passable for a trail bike, but only just.

"Don't you dare get me lost again," said Celia.

As an answer he held up an army compass for her to see. "Better than a ball of wool in a maze."

She tried to remember which Greek hero had found his way out of what labyrinth by marking his route with a ball of wool, and hurried after him down the track.

"I went left here," she said when they came to the fork. "Rosie was out of sight and I had to choose blind."

He grunted, looked at the map and took a compass bearing, then set off again down the right hand path. After meandering for a time on the level it dived steeply down towards the river and came out where a roaring waterfall plunged into a pool. Still bearing right it followed the river bank downstream for almost half a mile, then turned away from the water into a patch of scrub.

MacRae stopped. "I thought we'd end up here. This is where she was found."

Twigs had been broken off and the earth trampled by many feet. Otherwise it was just a patch of ground like any other. "Lying on her back," he said. "Seeing her like that made me damn angry, she was a splendid creature."

Celia forced herself to stop looking at the trampled earth. "She came here to meet someone."

"Stands to reason. She had a date with whoever shot her. But she took a funny route. Knew you were chasing after her, did she?"

"Possibly. I'm not sure."

"Must have known." He unfolded the map and jabbed at it. "Look, she starts off south-east. Get you on the wrong track and thoroughly lost, right? Then she heads off north to keep her date. Where? Not here, you need a landmark or you miss each other, Herne the Hunter's Oak, or the ruined chapel. It's no use saying 'meet me at another part of the forest', Shakespeare's people got in one hell of a muddle that way." He looked round. "There's no landmark here, this wasn't the meeting place."

"But the murderer didn't wait at the landmark. He came to meet her."

"No. Wrong direction. The Mount Ephraim gate's up there, he'd expect her to come that way. She came along the river bank because she'd made a detour to shake you off."

Celia puzzled this out. "Then whoever she's going to meet isn't the murderer and stays put at the rendezvous and a third party, who is, jumps out from behind the *Olearia haastii* shouting 'Ill met by moonlight, proud Titania'."

"Or words to that effect. Bang bang."

"Let's see where this path goes to," she suggested.

"Fishermen's track along the bank," he said, moving off. Presently a chance remark of Celia's revealed that fly fishing in England was a rich man's sport, with jealously guarded trout and salmon rivers.

"How can people live in a country like that?" he growled. "Here, anyone who takes out a license can fish wherever they like."

A mile farther on the path arrived at an S-bend in the river, where winter rains had built up a gravel pit. Rusting iron stove pipes and the bleached remains of wooden huts poked up among the low scrub on the bank.

"Here's our landmark, consisting of ruined fishermen's huts," said Celia.

"No. That gravel spit's gold-bearing dirt. They panned it in a thing called a Long Tom and the gold came to the top. These were their houses."

She poked around among the ruins. "If this is the rendezvous you'd expect footprints and eggshells and discarded soup tins."

"Hell no, you wait for the lady before you picnic."

"He spent the night here, surely? We were in that minibus before dawn, no one came past us up the gorge."

"Thornhill wouldn't need to," said MacRae. "He'd come down from Mount Ephraim."

"Can you see Rosie hurrying to an assignation with him? I can't. He's the murderer who jumps out of the bushes before she gets to the rendezvous. Tom, what's that over there?"

"Hebe armstrongii."

"I know that, behind the hebe."

A rectangle of yellowing grass showed where something flat had been lying till very recently. "About three feet square, Tom. Can you see it anywhere?"

A few yards away they found some rotting boards held together by a rusting hinge, possibly the remains of a window shutter. It had been arranged naturalistically over the traces of a recent camp fire.

"Lit a fire, then didn't want anyone to know he'd been," said MacRae. "Who, though? Stanley Parker would fit the bill. Mysterious feller, kept disappearing. Brent says he was in the township the night before."

"Brent says so because that's what he's been told, Tom. I'm supposed to have followed Parker from Christchurch like Donna Elvira snapping at the heels of Don Juan, so they had to say he'd been seen around. It may not be true, but in any case, whoever was here is the non-murderer with the assignation with Rosie."

"And on hearing a damn great bang, he behaves like the cares that infested Longfellow," said MacRae with a twinkle.

"Stop showing off and being difficult."

" 'He folded his tent like the Arab and silently stole away.' Ah, tent. That's an idea, let's see where he pitched it."

But before he could move Celia put a hand on his arm. "Sh! Listen. Voices."

They came from the wooded heights above them and were getting closer. Footsteps pounded down the slope with a rustle of fallen leaves. There were two speakers, both men. Soon movement could be seen, filtered through tree trunks. They had barely time to hide in the undergrowth behind a hoheria before Ed Moffat and Harry Watson appeared, coming straight towards them.

"This is the place," said Moffat, looking round among the wreckage of the gold-panners' huts. "The stuff's somewhere over there."

Frustratingly, the pair moved on out of sight behind a high clump of scrub.

"What sort of stuff?" asked Watson's deep voice.

"See for yourself, it's over there. Pup tent, stove, blanket, the usual things."

"Who found it?"

"Bill and Nobby, while they were searching for Rosie. They won't talk, come and have a look."

To Celia's fury, they moved away out of earshot.

"Anything to show whose it was, Ed?"

"No. It must have been Parker, who else?"

"An angler? Caching his stuff for when he comes back here?"

"He's not coming back, Harry. The blanket's got all his rubbish wrapped up in it, eggshells, soup tins, butter paper, the bones of some bird he cooked, it's enough to turn your stomach. You don't do that if you're coming back, you do it if you're getting the hell out of here and don't want anyone to know you've been."

"Why doesn't he bury the rubbish and take the rest with him?"

"He's on foot, Harry, travelling light. So what do we do? Drop the lot in the incinerator at your place? We don't want anyone to know he's been, any more than he does."

"I'm not sure of that, Ed."

"I am. I still say, keep the story simple. Rosie runs away in a panic and hides in the bush because dainty little Miss United Kingdom is after her in a rage with a gun. She catches up with Rosie and shoots her to punish her for stealing her lover. End of simple story, why do we need to bring the damn lover on stage?"

"Because dainty little Miss United Kingdom is a much tougher sheila than she looks. When Brent faced her with your simple story she treated him like he was some kind of ridiculous insect. It shook him, he's

beginning to have doubts. What if she can prove that she's never met Parker in her life?"

"What if Brent can prove that Thornhill shot Rosie? It's no use him saying he didn't, he looks as guilty as sin."

"Okay, we have to take the heat off Thornhill, but we don't have to make a cast-iron case against someone else. We can protect him by making a muddle, see? Cover that stuff up and leave it here. Let Brent find it and wonder whether it's Parker's, that'll keep his mind busy for days."

"What would Parker's motive be for shooting Rosie?"

"That's not our worry, let Brent use his imagination. Come on, let's go."

Celia pricked up her ears. They were coming back.

"I'm puzzled," Moffat was saying. "What was Parker doing, messing about for days in the gorge? All I know is, that bird-watching story was a phoney."

"Watching for black stilts, was it?" asked the gloomy Watson.

"So he said. They only breed in one place, on the upper Waikare, there's none round here."

Their voices faded away. "How much of that did you hear?" Celia asked.

"Very little. Where's this cache they found, let's look."

They found it in one of the pits which the gold-panners had dug for long-forgotten purposes, covered with an artistic arrangement of debris and bits of plank. MacRae pulled out the blanket and unfolded it.

"It's evidence, should you interfere?" said Celia.

122

"They did, so why shouldn't I? Here's his rubbish, let's look. Filthy mess, but here we are, bones of bird cooked and eaten by camper."

"What about them?"

"A problem of morbid anatomy, is this Kentucky Fried Chicken or something he shot? Oh no, not Kentucky Fried Chicken, too small and the wrong shape, possibly a kea. I wonder what it tasted like."

"What's a kea?"

"A sort of comic parrot. Anyway, we conclude that the camper had a gun."

"Can't one snare parrots?"

"Why? How?"

"I don't know, but poachers snare pheasants in England. Some arrangement with wire or string."

"Why not shoot them? Far less trouble."

"Because the gamekeepers would hear."

"Gamekeepers. My God, what a country, how can you exist there?"

"The camper isn't supposed to have a gun," said Celia. "Or were there two guns, one for him and one for the murderer in the bushes?"

Puzzling about this, they packed the blanket and its sordid contents back into their hiding place and started back to the car.

"You heard what Watson said?" Celia asked. "About Parker messing about in the gorge for days and pretending to watch for black stilts? He must have been planting out those rarities."

She was depressed. She had been clinging to the hope that the botanical fraud in the gorge was Bertie's work, and that she would somehow be able to trace

123

him through it. But Parker had elbowed Bertie right out of the picture.

"*Can't you find out?*"

"*No, Jim.*"

"*Why not? Why do we run a consular operation in Auckland if not for this sort of thing?*"

"*Why do our esteemed diplomatic colleagues in Wellington want to know?*"

"*Because my mother-in-law's been commissioned urgently by his family to find him. I've cleared it with H.E., he says please give me every co-operation.*"

"*I daresay, but we're up to our necks here in distressed British seamen. Can't your mother-in-law wait?*"

"*No, and H.E. has ruled that Lord Albert Melton's presence in New Zealand is not conducive to good Commonwealth relations, and he's to be found and shipped off home pronto.*"

"*My dear Jim, he can't be shipped home, the Kiwis have confiscated his passport.*"

"*Let me get this story straight. You say he was detained at Sydney Airport on suspicion of smuggling. Why only suspicion, and smuggling what?*"

"*God knows. The Narcotics people are handling it, and you know how tight-lipped they are.*"

"*Into or out of Australia?*"

"*Into, apparently. He arrived at Sydney on a flight from Auckland, and the Aussies, having discovered whatever they did discover, put him on the next flight back here. They do tend to dump undesirables on poor little New Zealand whenever they can.*"

"*And what have the Kiwis done with him?*"

"They won't say. I only know about it because my contact in Narcotics rang and asked me what I knew about the old nuisance. When I asked about the whys and wherefores they told me the bare minimum."

"Is he in prison?"

"No, they took his passport and I suppose told him to report daily to the police. My guess is that they turned him loose hoping he'd lead them to bigger fry, and he shook off whoever was tailing him and now they're too embarrassed to say they've lost him."

"In which case he's loose in New Zealand without a passport, exerting his high-octane nuisance value. What a delightful scenario, H.E. and my mother-in-law will be pleased."

Brent was still using the schoolhouse as an office. He had barricaded himself in behind the teacher's desk and was glowering over it at Celia and MacRae.

"Surely you see the point," she told him. "Traces of a camp have been found within a mile of where Mrs Murphy was shot. They were found by two men called Bill and Nobby during the search for her. They didn't see fit to mention this very relevant circumstance to the police, and we both heard Ed Moffat remarking that they could be trusted to hold their tongue. Why keep it secret? You would do well to ask."

"You're making a very serious accusation against a respected local citizen," said Brent. "What proof have I that Mr Moffat really said it?"

"We both heard it," said MacRae. "You have two independent witnesses."

Brent gave a lewd smirk. "Independent?"

"Young man, what are you suggesting?" thundered

Celia in a voice like hailstones. She had discovered that shouting at him was a sure-fire way of making him say something silly.

This he proceeded to do. "You're an attractive woman, Mrs Grant, and you spent most of last evening in Dr MacRae's motel room."

"You little bastard," MacRae roared. "Just because you follow your testicles around in a randy daze, that doesn't mean everyone else does. Sorry, Celia, that was a bit rude."

"Think nothing of it, I was about to point out to the Inspector that some people's motivation originates above the waistline."

Brent burst out in a rage. "You come to me with fantastic stories about prominent local people—"

"—And prominent local people come to you with fantastic stories about me," Celia interrupted.

"You want to solve this case?" said MacRae. "Or are you so terrified of offending these prominent local people that you're pushing all the worms back into their cans and ramming the lids on?"

"There are no cans of worms," Brent shouted.

Speaking alternately, like a Greek chorus, Celia and MacRae explained where the worms should be looked for, but this only enraged him further. No one, he said, was telling him how to run his investigation. Baby or no baby, Celia was not leaving till her part of the affair was cleared up.

"Which will be never at the present rate of progress," she objected. "Must I sit here till Doomsday while you refuse to believe a word I say?"

"If you try to leave here without my permission, Mrs Grant, I shall have you arrested."

"On what charge? Murder? Think twice before you do that, any competent lawyer would make mincemeat of your evidence and you."

She escaped, and stood trembling on the steps of the schoolhouse. A reaction had set in. She had been far too rude, Brent would massacre her.

"I must have been mad, Tom. He'll keep me here forever now, to punish me."

"Don't get too fussed about Brent," said MacRae. "He can be fixed."

"Really, how?"

"I'll ring someone who can sort him out, make him see sense."

"A friend of yours?"

"We were cobbers in the army."

Male reliance on the efficiency of old-boy networks always astonished Celia, who did not share it. Nevertheless she submitted meekly and let herself be guided into his motel room, which proved to be full of tweedy pipe-smoking botanists, lying about on the floor at all angles: friends of his, summoned to give a verdict on the "rarities". After introducing her round, he vanished, presumably to phone the friend who was supposed to sort Brent out.

Her entrance caused a stir. She was much more conscious of herself as a woman in a roomful of men than she would have been in England, and so, it seemed, were they. After compliments on her alertness in raising the alarm, they returned to the problem they had been discussing: what should be done with an important collection of rare plants which had no business to be where they were? By rights they should be lifted and removed before they seeded themselves and distorted the natural pattern of plant distribution, but to dig up and re-pot plants on the endangered list while they were in flower would endanger them still further. . . . MacRae seemed to be away a long time. His sorting out of Brent was probably getting nowhere. It was awful to have come right round the world for a daughter's first baby and not be there.

More time passed. The ecological seminar had degenerated into catty gossip at the expense of botanical pundits who had sounded off with indignant trumpetings against the dam on the strength of Marano's say-so. She could bear it no longer. Muttering an excuse, she fled towards the camper, feeling very miserable indeed.

But as she fled she ran slap into a hard male stomach surmounted, high above her, by Lance Johnson's pink face and sandy hair. "Hi Celia, I'm having trouble," he announced.

She took a grip on herself and managed not to say: "*You* are!"

"The thing was kept very quiet, the family had a lot of influence. She came from Hawkes Bay, that's all I know."

Celia remembered now. She had asked him to find out for her the name and whereabouts of the nymphet who had figured in the Ted Murphy sex scandal.

"All we have to go on is Thornhill's statement in parliament that Murphy had got an under-age girl pregnant and ought to resign because left-wing ideas always led to immorality and drugs and what all."

"How d'you know she came from Hawkes Bay?" Celia asked.

"It was a Hastings lawyer did the fixing, to keep it out of the papers. He acts for a lot of those awesome Hawkes Bay families who came over with the Twelve Apostles."*

"The people the lawyer fixed must know."

"That's right, I have a contact there who's working on it. Fair's fair though. I'm going to a lot of trouble to get you this information, let's have some reciprocity. Why d'you want to know?"

Celia pointed out that he had already had his reciprocity in the form of Sir Edward Bolton, and if he wanted more information he would have to do something else for her: go to Christchurch airport and find out if anyone apart from Watson's hired hand claimed to have seen Parker arrive there. Did any of the taxi drivers remember picking her up and taking her on a round of car hire firms, and if so how soon after her plane landed? Had anyone seen her quarrelling with Parker?

"It's quite a small airport, so the staff will probably remember," she ended. "The story's nonsense, of course, but I'd like it to be disproved."

"Okay, it's a deal. Now tell me why you're interested in Murphy's nymphet."

"That's a long story."

"I like long stories." He opened the door of his motel unit. "Come in and I'll fix you a drink."

"Thank you, but may we leave the door open? I've already been accused of immoral relations with Dr MacRae."

*A nickname for the Founding Fathers of the town of Hastings.

He hooted with laughter. "With that old identity? Oh *no!*"

"I don't know why you think it's funny," she said coldly, and launched into the "long story" by reminding him of Thornhill's nose-bleed in the woolshed, and the drama of Rosie's handkerchief.

"That whole episode was bizarre," he commented. "Thornhill tried to get the TV people to edit it out of the news coverage. We thought he didn't want to be seen accepting so much as a handkerchief from the opposition."

Celia started to explain his real motive, but Johnson interrupted. "Hold it. I'm getting this exclusive, right? You're not giving it to the others?"

She assured him that this was so, and he sat down where he could watch the approaches to the open door. "Just in case of eavesdropping by the opposition."

Celia went on with her story, but suddenly Johnson was not paying attention. A shadow from the light on the porch outside had fallen across the threshold. Someone was indeed eavesdropping. He tiptoed to the door and was about to pounce when the shadow moved away. He grabbed, and pulled the eavesdropper into the room.

"Who the hell are you? Who d'you represent?"

Surprisingly, the eavesdropper was not a journalist, but a simply dressed middle-aged woman. "Shut the door, I mustn't be seen," she murmured.

"What were you doing out there?" Johnson asked.

"I wanted to find out if anyone was with her. There was, so I was going away."

When she realized that Johnson was a newspaperman she panicked. After a lot of hesitation and reassurance, she said that her name was Mrs Wooton and that it wasn't right, someone had to speak out, despite the risk to those who spoke out of turn. What risk, Celia asked. "A gap cut in your wire so that your stock gets out, nasty phone calls, a savage dog set on your sheep . . ."

Celia asked who was behind these unpleasantnesses, but this was too scary a question to answer. "I'll say what I came to tell you, then go."

The Wootons were small farmers. She and her husband had been doing their weekly shop in Crampton's store when two of the hired hands from Derwent came in. "Reg and Pete Jackson, they were no good even as boys, really nasty, not just wild. They were buying a roll of number eight . . ."

"Fencing wire," Johnson interjected.

With typical fecklessness, the Jacksons had started repairing a break in the Derwent perimeter fence without first making sure they had enough wire, and had to drive down to the township to buy more. When the Wootons left the shop, Reg and Pete were loading their wire into a utility, and Pete, opening the cab door, had said: "Where's the gun?"

"And Reg said, you must have left it up by the fence where we were working, and Pete said he was sure he hadn't and never took it out of the cab, and there was quite an argument."

"What time was all this?" Celia asked.

"It's not what time, dear, it's *which day*. That's why I had to speak. It's all over the township that you're supposed to have stolen the gun to shoot poor Mrs

Murphy with, but how could you when it was missing a whole day before?"

"Let me get this straight," said Celia. "When did all this happen?"

"On the Wednesday morning, dear. The day before she was shot."

Celia went over to her and gave her a great hug. "Mrs Wooten, I can't thank you enough for being so brave and coming forward."

"I had to, dear. It's all very well shutting one's eyes to dishonest goings-on. One can't let an innocent person be arrested for murder."

"Are you going to be even braver and tell Inspector Brent what you've told me?"

Panic set in again. "They're watching him to see who he talks to. Wooton said it would be okay for me to slip over here in the dark after the bible class, and you could tell Brent. If he wants to talk to us, he must come to our place after dark and not in a police car. Promise me, won't you?"

Johnson had another try at making her say who was behind the threats, but to no avail. After more assurances of secrecy she left, insisting that the light in the room should be put out before the door was opened.

"I hope she comes to no harm," said Celia. As an extra precaution she did not betray her excitement by rushing to Brent with the news, but phoned Wellington first.

It was Jim who answered, not Lucy. Before she could speak, he launched into his tale of woe about Bertie.

"Smuggling?" she echoed when the full scale of the disaster had been explained to her. "*Into* Australia? Smuggling what, for heaven's sake?"

Jim told her what he knew.

"Hell's bells," said Celia. "Hermione will burst a blood vessel when I tell her."

"She rang here this morning. When are you coming back?"

"I'm not sure. Don't tell Lucy, it might worry her, but a very stupid policeman suspects me of shooting Rosie. It's ludicrous, and I've just got a piece of evidence that clears me completely, but he'll take days checking it, so I don't know when I'll get away. Oh dear, if I'm absent from the birth-pangs on top of everything else, the success of my New Zealand visit will be complete."

He started to say it would not matter if she missed the birth, but was in danger of implying that she might as well have stayed home and changed the subject hastily. "You asked me to trace Rosie's secretary. She's on holiday in Tahiti—"

"How helpful she would be."

"—But I've found a woman who used to be her husband's secretary, would she be of any use?"

"She might be worth trying, if I can ever get away from this place."

"You will eventually. If you came by train you could call on her on your way back here." He gave her the name and address, then called Lucy to the phone. To Celia's distressed imagination she sounded like a small child very far away, trying not to sound frightened.

"I'm fine Mum. I'm sure it's going to be a daring little revolutionary like Trotsky or Rosa Luxemburg. Whenever haughty Mrs High Commissioner calls to show how caring senior foreign service wives are, it kicks like a mule."

Brent was lodging at the hotel. Made desperate by Lucy's plight, Celia marched into it boldly, cut through a crowd of astonished men, and asked at the bar to see him. The landlord hurried her aside into a frowsty parlour, where she was presently joined by Brent, smelling of beer.

"Now, look here, Inspector," she began.

He held up a hand. "I was about to send you a message. The police have no objection to you leaving Kirkstone, provided you keep us informed of your address."

His voice was thick with fury. This was no change of heart, he had been overruled from above. Tom MacRae's old-boy net had produced results after all.

She thanked Brent politely and told him of Mrs Wooton's statement about the gun. He listened sulkily, and said, without sounding very interested, that he would investigate. Celia tried to make her way out of the hotel. But many of the customers were pressmen, who blocked her path and shouted questions at her. After several minutes of this she was rescued by Johnson, who picked her up and carried her out of the building, informing all concerned that she was his exclusive property. She thanked him for rescuing her and told him where to get in touch with her in Wellington.

"Brent's letting you leave?" he asked.

"Tom MacRae fixed it. He rang someone he knew, an old friend from the army. Who on earth can it have been?"

"Anyone from the Minister of Justice down, this is the New Zealand Division mafia at work."

The New Zealand Division. Of course, he was the right age. He would have been nineteen, twenty at most when he and the "cobber" set out across the world to fight their way from the outskirts of Cairo to Venice in defence of a mother country they had never seen. The cobber had become the sort of policeman who could make inspectors jump to attention and Tom had become a country doctor, but the network still operated.

"I must go and thank him," she said.

Johnson made a face. "Got tickets on you, has he? Pity, he's too old for you."

"I'm not sure what you mean, and anyway it's none of your business, Mr Johnson. Goodnight."

MacRae was alone. He opened the door, grinning broadly. "Didn't believe me, did you? I told you I'd fix it. You'll be off in the morning, when will I see you again?"

"I don't know, Tom."

"If I flew up to Wellington, would you come out to a lunch or a tea with me?"

"Oh dear, I'd be very embarrassed if you made the journey specially. I like you a lot, and if we lived in the same place I'm sure we'd be very close friends. But we don't, my roots are on the other side of the world—"

"You could grow roots here."

"I'm sorry, Tom. I know people with roots at both

ends. Most of them are miserable whichever end they are, and spend their lives scraping up the fare to get to the other."

"If I write, will you answer?"

"Of course, and thank you for all you've done."

She went back sadly to the camper. He was amusing and intelligent and kind. The same age as Roger would be if he was alive. But he was not Roger.

❧ SEVEN ❧

The train pulled out of Christchurch station and headed north into classy suburbs with swimming pools in their gardens. Celia collapsed in her seat, exhausted. Everyone had told her she would love Christchurch, it was just like an English cathedral city, but there had been no time for love. She had caught the train by minutes, after an obstacle race up the steps of a pompously municipal railway station to reach the platforms, where the rails seemed strangely close together; an arrangement which perhaps accounted for the rather bumpy ride.

Despite the last-minute rush she had managed to buy all three Christchurch papers. As the train chugged slowly across a rich agricultural plain she nerved herself to riffle through them. The reporting from Kirkstone was very guarded. The journalists had picked their way carefully through the twin minefields of libel and contempt of court, but anyone reading between the lines would realise that attractive petite Ceila Grant was the prime suspect. What unnerved her most were the photos of her grimacing hideously, like attractive petite Lucrezia Borgia about to commit her twentieth murder.

The *Post*, Lance Johnson's paper, had the biggest headline of all; RARE PLANTS A FAKE, SAYS UK BOTANIST. She scanned the text eagerly. ". . . No plant more than three years old . . . growing at altitudes where they are not usually found. . . . A strict ecological code which forbids introducing into the wild cultivated specimens which might give a false picture of the plant's natural distribution . . ." Quite, Celia thought, but what have they found out in Sydney? The answer came halfway down the column:

. . . The plants in question could not have been obtained from New Zealand sources without the matter coming to the knowledge of botanical experts. Where, then, did they come from?

DARK DEALINGS IN AUSTRALIA

I learn exclusively that the widow of Sir Edward Bolton, who died in October at his home in Sydney, was approached early in November by a man giving his name as Parkinson, whose description corresponds exactly with that of a man known in Kirkstone as Parker, who has recently been a frequent house guest of the late Rose Murphy, and who is said to have spent much time in the area where the rare plants were found, on the pretext of bird-watching. Sir Edward was an enthusiastic grower of rare New

Zealand plants, and "Parkinson" persuaded Lady Bolton to sell him a large number of choice specimens from her husband's collection.

A STRANGE COINCIDENCE

The list of plants sold to "Parkinson" by Lady Bolton is identical with that of the alleged rarities found in the Kirkstone area, with the exception of one dwarf clematis which has not been found there, presumably because it did not survive transplanting from its pot to the open mountainside. Enquiries at the Department of Agriculture have established that no import licence was granted for these plants, which must therefore have been smuggled into the country. This discovery only deepens the mystery surrounding the death of Rose Murphy, who . . .

The rest of the story was on familiar lines, except that Celia looked quite human in the picture, and was not described more or less openly as a murderess. It was vexing, though, that all this confirmed Parker in his role as the provider and planter-out of the false rarities. How, then, did Bertie fit in? What had he been smuggling into Australia while Parker was smuggling the plants out?

The train, which had been chugging through lowland sheep country, suddenly started to run along an enchanted coast of rocks and sand and brilliant blue sea, with wading birds picking about in the shallows and even a lonely seal basking on a rock. Celia scowled at the seal in a black mood of self-pity. She ought to have stayed in Kirkstone to see what nonsense was being stuffed into Brent's head and extract as much of it as possible. Hermione would slaughter her for not going to Auckland at once to bully the truth about Bertie out of the Narcotics people. If she was anywhere but Wellington when the baby arrived she would be branded as an unnatural grandmother. But how the hell could she be in all these places at once?

Cursing her lot and eating railway sandwiches, she fell into a heavy sleep of exhaustion. When she woke the train had swung away from the coast into a landscape of treeless, scalped-looking hills where sheep grazed with disgusted expressions, as if an unvaried diet of grass had begun to pall. After an hour or more of this, the train drew into Picton, where she was to be met and taken to see Ted Murphy's ex-secretary.

The ferry was at the pier, ready for the three-and-a-half-hour journey down Queen Charlotte's sound and across Cook's Strait to Wellington. Haunted by visions of the baby arriving at that very moment, she was strongly tempted to board the ferry. But it was too late.

"Mrs Grant? I'm Janey Matthew's nephew, my name's Tim. Let me take your case."

"Thank you. How clever of you to pick me out in this crowd."

"Your son-in-law gave me a detailed description, and if I may say so you live up to it. The boat's down in by the jetty, it's this way."

He installed her in the stern of a boat with an outboard motor and headed down the sound. He was youngish, late twenties perhaps, and wore a wedding ring. It turned out that he was staying with his aunt for the holidays with his wife and children, a girl of four and a boy of eight months. But he seemed embarrassed by questions about them and changed the subject so abruptly that she wondered if one of them was handicapped. The scenery was spectacular, a fiord-like pattern of inlets and islands with an abandoned whaling station rotting quietly in the sun and a flock of gulls busy over a shoal of fish. An arctic skua was attacking them one by one and making them disgorge their fish, which it caught in mid-air and swallowed.

Tim steered the boat round a promontory and tied up at a small landing stage with steps leading upwards to a pine chalet with a wide porch, the holiday cottage of Ted Murphy's ex-secretary. She was waiting at the top of the steps, an overweight middle-aged woman with the baby on her arm and the older child clinging to her skirts.

"Hi Celia, I'm Janey Matthews," she said. "My, what pretty hair and look at that figure, how do you manage it?"

"I diet like a dervish one week in every month," said Celia, telling her usual lie. The truth ("I eat like a horse and to hell with it") made fat women want to tear her limb from limb.

"I could kill you for envy, but never mind, siddown and let's hear what's on your mind. Sarah!"

The children's mother came round the corner of the house.

"Meet Celia, love," said Janey, "and would you take these two darling loads of trouble round the back. Celia and I have to talk."

With the children gone, they settled down in long chairs on the porch.

"As you'll have gathered from broad hints in the newspapers," Celia began, "everyone but me seems to think I shot Rose Murphy."

"You didn't? You look cool and clever enough, and she made lots of enemies." Janey gave a loud fat-woman's laugh. "I'm awful, don't mind me, I say the first thing that comes into my head. If you didn't, who did?"

"I think I know. And I think it all began with something that happened in Kirkstone in her husband's lifetime."

Janey's defences went up at once. "I'm sorry, I only worked for him in Wellington, I don't know what went on up there at their summer place."

"I see, but let me ask you all the same. I think he got to know about some suspicious goings-on in and around Kirkstone, and perhaps threatened to ask awkard questions in parliament. D'you remember anything like that?"

The defences came down again. This was not the question that Janey had expected, or feared. She concentrated, but could suggest nothing.

"It would probably have been something to do with two men called Ed Moffat and Harry Watson, they're the managers of two state farms at the top of the Kirkstone Valley."

"Oh. Wait. What were the names of the farms?"

"Mount Shelly, which is a cattle breeding station, and Derwent, which is a deer ranch."

"There *was* something about this, early last year. Ted had been through the accounts of those two farms, they were making huge losses that the taxpayer was having to meet and he couldn't see why. And there was something more, I remember now. He was trying to charter a light plane to fly him over the top of the valley.''

"Why?''

"I've no idea, but he wanted me to fix it and the local air charter company up there kept making excuses and putting him off, and he got very suspicious about that.''

"Did he ever find out what was going on?''

"No.''

"I think I know why not. He was too worried to follow it up because the next thing that happened was the trouble over that girl, am I right?''

"Yes.'' The defences were up again with a vengeance. This was the no-go area that had to be protected.

"Didn't you realize what had happened?'' Celia asked. "Someone set a honey-trap for him and started the sex scandal to make him harmless.''

"It wasn't a trap,'' said Janey fiercely. "She was just a randy little bitch. She couldn't take care of herself and got into trouble and Thornhill found out and made a meal of it.''

"Rosie was convinced it was a trap.''

"Oh, her,'' said Janey acidly.

"D'you know the name of the girl?''

"Yes, but she's trying to make a fresh start. I don't tell anyone her name or where she is.''

"Fair enough, but did she have any connection with Moffat or Watson or anyone in the Kirkstone Valley?''

"I don't know," shouted Janey, going brick red with the effort of lying.

"What happened to the baby, is her family looking after it?"

"Why d'you want to know?" she shouted even louder. "Why are you asking all these questions?"

"Because I'm likely to be arrested on a trumped-up charge of murder unless I find out what's going on. Was it a boy or a girl?"

"A boy," said Janey, rigid in her long chair.

Suddenly Celia saw what this was all about. Tim had changed the subject abruptly when she asked him about the children, and what an odd family, a girl of four and then a long gap. Eight months too. The right age.

"The baby's here, isn't he?" she said. "I saw him just now."

Without warning Janey relaxed and became a fat jolly woman again. "It's a big hoot, isn't it? Thank God I can laugh at myself, I'm a stock comic character, the fat slob of a middle-aged secretary carrying a torch for her employer and even looking after his illegit."

"I'm not laughing, I'm impressed," said Celia. "You arranged for Tim and Sarah to adopt him?"

"That's right, luckily I had a legacy I could pass on to them. If it had been a girl I'd have taken the job on myself, but a boy needs a father."

Careful now, Celia thought. There was one more question to be cleared up, but the answer lay in an emotional minefield. "Did Mrs Murphy take an interest in the baby? He is her stepson."

"No. She couldn't be bothered with children, that's why she didn't give Ted any."

"But she knew what you'd arranged?"

"I told her about the adoption, yes."

"But she didn't keep in touch through you with Tim and Sarah?"

"Not till a month ago. She phoned me, said she'd found some things of Ted's that she wanted his son to have, and what was the address. I gave it her, but she didn't send anything."

"And since then, has there been any . . . attack on the baby, an accident, anything that drew blood?"

"Yes! You frighten me Celia, how did you know, are you clairvoyant?"

"No. I'll explain, but tell me first what happened."

"He was in his pram in their front garden in Wellington and Sarah was hanging out washing round the back when she heard him scream. About a month ago, it was, there was a big panic with inoculations and all, they thought a cat had scratched him."

"It wasn't a cat, it was Rosie," said Celia. "She was collecting blood samples, trying to prove that the baby wasn't her husband's child."

Janey sat up sharply in her chair. "That's nonsense, you don't believe it?"

". . . What worries me is that Rosie did."

"He's Ted's child. He has a look of Ted."

Celia said nothing. It would be too cruel to tell her about the moment of truth when Rose Murphy realized that Thornhill was afraid to let her have a blood sample.

"You'll stay to tea?" said Janey far from warmly.

"Thank you, but I have to get to Wellington," Celia replied, as eager to go as Janey was to get rid of her.

"I'll tell Tim to take you back to Picton," said Janey. "Promise not to tell him what you've just told me."

"Lance, you lazy lout, where are you?"

"Kirkstone. Where else?"

"Shagging with that pommy blonde with the big boobs, I bet."

"Her knockers are nothing special and there are no gold hairs among the silver."

"So you say."

"Jeff, you ran her picture yesterday, have a look at it. Anyway, she left this morning for Wellington."

"Lance, I want you back here."

"Listen, I'm on to another big exclusive for you."

"The last one was exclusive for all of two hours. Then a massed chorus of botanists began calling Marano unbotanical names and telling the agencies the damn plants were phonies. Get back here, the story's three days old. It's inside-page stuff."

"It'll get a lot bigger before it's through."

"If it does we'll use agency coverage."

"The agencies aren't getting the story. This is Frightsville, people are afraid to talk."

"Or just bored by your questions. Who would they be afraid of?"

"Thornhill, for one."

"The MP? This sounds like a load of brightly coloured balls to me."

"He could have killed Rosie. I've traced his movements that day. At ten o'clock he was up at Mount Ephraim, one of the agency men phoned him there for

a quote on the shindig in the woolshed the night before. Rosie was up there in the Mount Ephraim woods by ten-thirty, and Thornhill was down in Kirkstone an hour after that, allegedly buying sheep dip at the store. He could have shot her on the way down."

"Why would he want to do that?"

"I told you, he's the father of the child in the Murphy sex scandal and he's afraid Rosie can prove it. So he shoots her and comes down to the township to break into her house and ransack it for that blood-stained handkerchief."

"Watched by the terrified inhabitants of Frights-ville, who pretend to each other that in his haste to secure sheep dip he has mistaken Rosie's house for the store."

"He was around in the township for quite a while, he could have broken in there at the back."

"Is this your theory, or is it guilty Mrs Big-knockers leading you around by the nose?"

"She was right about the plants coming from that garden in Australia, she was right about Rosie sending blood samples for analysis, and she knows a lot she hasn't told me."

"For instance?"

"There's something about a Lord Albert Melton, Brent was asking people if they'd seen him in the township, but he won't say why. According to botanical circles he's a sort of flower-mad nuisance who appears every so often from the UK. He may have something to do with the phoney rarities, I bet she knows how he fits in."

"Ask her, for cripes sake."

"I did, she says business is business, she'll tell me when I give her the name of the nymphet in the Murphy sex scandal. What are they doing about that in Hastings? Ring them and say I need it soonest."

"Ring them yourself."

"Can't. Someone's just had a working dog battered to death, and I know who did it and why. I told you, this place is Frightsville."

"I am *not* panicking," said Lucy tetchily. "I just think I should have been told, that's all."

It was mid-afternoon. Below the balcony Wellington harbour shone like a blue mirror. Even under the awning it was very hot.

"I felt such a fool, hearing it from her," Lucy added.

Hermione had phoned while Celia was still in transit on the ferry, and had told Lucy by way of casual conversation that her mother was about to be arrested for murder.

"I'm sorry Lucy love, I thought I wouldn't bother you with it just before you hatch out. The whole thing's a farce, there's a policeman there who believes in sex with everything and he's invented a huge fat lover for me, it would be a nightmare. Like poor little Atlas balancing the world on top of himself."

"Your policeman kept phoning, sounding angrier and angrier. At first I couldn't think why."

"I suppose I should ring him and calm him down," Celia murmured, but did not move. The air was drowsy and the long chair high above the water was seductive. She was half asleep when the phone shattered her calm.

"That'll be him, he rings every hour," said Lucy.

It was indeed Brent. He was incoherent with rage and kept accusing her of having left Kirkstone "under false pretences", a phrase which he refused to explain, saying she knew perfectly well what he meant. She was to come back at once and report to him.

"Inspector, you should see a psychiatrist, you are obviously unwell," said Celia and put the phone down. She had scarcely settled down again on the balcony when it rang again.

"My turn," said Lucy and heaved herself up.

"If it's him again, say I've gone out."

But the call was from Tom MacRae. "Celia? Thought I'd better warn you, Brent's gone off his nut."

"Yes. He was on the line just now. What's all this about false pretences?"

"The Wootons have taken fright and gone back on what they said. No, they didn't hear Moffat's men say where was the gun, no they didn't tell you anything like that, they can't imagine what the Inspector is on about. They're terrified."

"Why?"

"Their huntaway was clubbed to death last night, just as a warning."

"Oh dear, what is a huntaway please?"

"A working dog that rushes around making the hell of a row to move the sheep from one pasture to the next; as opposed to an eye dog, which does the job by glaring silently in a sitting posture like the sphinx. Brent thinks you invented the Wooton story and fed it to higher authority through me, as a plot to get away from Kirkstone."

What puzzled Celia was who had given the Wootons away to whoever killed their dog.

"That's a mystery," said MacRae. "News gets around quickly here, and I don't understand how. Why don't I take a trip to Wellington to come and see you?"

It took her a long time to get him off the phone.

For the next few days she concentrated on the domestic arts. The only event of interest was a call from Lance Johnson of the Christchurch *Post*. He was in Wellington and claimed to have much to tell her, but tried to trade his information against a promise that she would dine with him. When she refused to leave Lucy for a whole evening he settled for a drink, and they met in the lounge of what proved to be a superior hotel near Parliament Building.

"Very swept up," he apologized. "But a lot of the bars are a bit embarrassing for women."

"Swept up" seemed to be a term of abuse directed at the carpet, the flowers on the tables and the soft music, all symbols of an effete pretentiousness alien to New Zealand's pioneering spirit.

They settled in a corner. "I've gone to a lot of trouble for you, Celia," he began. "Be a bit nice to me, will you?" So saying, he plumped a hot hand down on hers, which he began massaging amorously.

"Come come, Mr Johnson," she said primly, freeing herself. "The editorial casting-couch is no place for a grandmother-to-be. Come on now, you're only doing it out of curiosity, to see how I react."

This proved to be a tactical error. He protested furiously that his dishonourable intentions were seriously meant, and tried to take her hand again. It took her some time to talk her way out of this erotic quagmire and persuade him to get down to business.

"The girl in the Murphy sex scandal is in the UK," he began.

This explained something that had always baffled Celia: why had Rosie interrupted her campaign to clear her husband's name to take a trip to England? Not to woo Bertie for the sake of his plants, that had been an afterthought. She had gone to collect a blood sample from the mother of his alleged child.

"Her name's Sandra Derbinsky," Johnson went on. "Not from one of the old-established Hastings families, they're Dallies."

Dallies, he explained were immigrants from Dalmatia on the Yugoslav coast. "Like most of the Hawkes Bay Dallies, the Derbinsky's are wine and fruit growers, but they're exceptionally rich. They farm a huge acreage and their Cabernet Sauvignon is supposed to be pretty special, and they have a damn great mansion in Havelock North and a holiday home in the Bay of Islands and everything you can think of in the way of cars and boats. And of course little fifteen-year-old Sandra thought all this far too bourgeois and school was a bore, and she was getting restive below the waistline, so she ran away with a garage hand and had to be hauled back from some kind of semi-brothel in Palmerston North and boarded out in disgrace where she couldn't come to harm, which was guess where."

"In Kirkstone."

"Yes, but where in Kirkstone?"

"The Moffats?"

"How did you guess?"

"Mrs Moffat had a foreign accent that I didn't recognize."

"That's right, she's a poor relation of the Derbinsky's," said Johnson. "Little Sandra was supposed to be out of harm's way on that ranch miles from anywhere, but they underrated her. Thornhill, then Ted Murphy. Two MPs. Wow!"

"Moffat and Watson may have pushed her in Thornhill's direction to get a blackmailing hold over him. If the affairs of those two farms don't bear looking into, they could do with one."

"The embarrassing baby that got palmed off on Murphy may not have been Thornhill's," Johnson suggested. "It could be the garage hand's. Or Moffat's."

"Not Moffat's, his blood group's wrong. Rosie established that. Anyway, the girl's in England now."

"That's right, Celia, her family packed her off there as soon as she'd had the baby, to a very swept-up boarding school."

"Which one?"

"I don't know, but if you want to trace her you probably can. Her parents are spreading it round that she's just won a scholarship to Cambridge." He eyed her, as if wondering whether to paw at her again. "Okay, that's my side of the bargain."

"Only part of it. What did you find out at Christchurch airport?"

"My God, Celia, you do insist on your pound and a half of flesh."

"Where information is concerned I am carnivorous, yes. Do go on."

"Okay then, okay. None of the staff at the airport remembers anyone corresponding to Parker's description, not surprising considering the number of people they see. Your taxi driver remembers you, but none of them took a fat man with a beard into town. One of them says he had an oldish fare with a beard who came off the plane before yours, but he was thin."

He paused and looked at her, puzzled. "Celia, why don't you like me?"

"Oh, but I do."

"Then why aren't you nice to me, like you were to old Tom MacRae?"

"What d'you mean, 'nice'?"

He was looking amorous again, and light suddenly dawned on Celia. "I see now what the trouble is. Inspector Brent, who has sex on what he probably thinks of as his brain, has been spreading it around that I'm what's vulgarly known as an easy lay, is that it? Oh dear, I see that I'm right, you may well blush. He did say something silly about me and Dr MacRae and I didn't think he believed it, but if he's been telling everyone . . . Good gracious, you didn't fly up to Wellington specially, inflamed with desire?

"Not exactly but—oh gosh, I'm sorry, I don't know what to say."

"Don't worry, now that sex is out of the way we can put our heads together and keep the rest of our anatomies apart."

"Oh gosh, I'm sorry," he repeated, squirming.

"Forget it and tell me, have you any idea what this criminal enterprise is that Moffat and Watson are involved in? That's what puzzles me the most."

"Strangely enough, yes, and I'm so embarrassed that I'm going to give you the information for free, without asking for reciprocity." He produced a batch of photographs from a battered brief case. "These were sent to me anonymously, and I flew up to check with the Agriculture Department here. Have a look."

The top picture was an air photo of a clearing in a forest with a small farm in it. There were enclosures containing cattle and what looked like deer and a range of farm buildings.

"Turn it over," said Johnson.

On the back of the print was a stuck-on typewritten caption: MOUNT EPHRAIM, UPPER KIRKSTONE VALLEY. THE FARM THAT ISN'T THERE, OR WHY DERWENT AND MOUNT SHELLEY DON'T MAKE A PROFIT.

There was another air photo, an oblique taken from a greater height. Johnson pointed with a pencil. "See the track going into the bush? It comes out of the trees again here, heading towards the Derwent boundary fence, there must be a Taranaki gate in it somewhere. That's the way they drive the stock along from the two state farms when they steal them. For accounting purposes they're written off as dead or not born or whatever."

The remaining photos had been taken from the ground; a general view of the same range of farm buildings, deer in a paddock, a group of cattle, the interior of a shed.

"That's the slaughterhouse," said Johnson. "The venison alone must sell for a bomb in America and West Germany, and have a look at these cattle. A pure-bred Ayrshire heifer like that would fetch five figures."

Other pictures were more puzzling; a typewriter with a second close-up shot showing its serial number, and similar pairs of photos showing the serial numbers of a chest deepfreeze, a TV set and various pieces of agricultural equipment. "Written off as defective and beyond repair at Derwent or Mount Shelley," Johnson explained, then frowned indignantly over some studies of long narrow tanks full of running water. "They've even been farming trout!"

"Is that very wrong?" Celia asked.

"It's illegal. We've a very powerful anglers' lobby here, they got it banned on the excuse that farmed trout would catch diseases and give them to wild trout. I'm astonished at a man like Thornhill getting mixed up in a sordid thing like this. The money's peanuts to him, he's one of the richest men in South Island. Why did he do it?"

"I suspect that he had no choice, because Watson and Moffat were blackmailing him over Sandra Derbinsky. That's why they set the honey-trap for him, they needed a remote corner of his land to hide their farm in."

Johnson thought about this. "You're probably right, but that still leaves Thornhill with the strongest motive for shooting Rosie. He knows she's on to him over the Derbinsky business, and if that can of worms gets opened God knows what else will come out."

"Will you be going back to Kirkstone?"

"Sure, as soon as I've got the Agriculture Department reaction to these pictures."

"When you do, have all the rooms in that motel checked for hidden microphones. It belongs to Crampton who owns the store, and he's in with Moffat and Watson, who would want to keep tabs on strangers passing through. I think that's how they found out that Mrs Wooton tipped us off about when the gun went missing."

"God, Celia, why aren't you an investigative reporter?"

"I can't type and I haven't the patience, but I do enjoy a mystery."

"I'd like to speak to the headmistress."

"Certainly, Your Grace, I'll put you through to Miss Vernon-Westcourt."

". . . Good afternoon, Duchess. What can I do for you?"

"You've a girl at the school called Sandra Derbinsky, her mother's a very old friend of mine. I was delighted to see from The Times *that she's landed a scholarship at Girton, clever girl."*

"Yes. Sandra has a good brain when she chooses to apply it."

"Well, they're often a bit dreamy at that age, aren't they?"

"I wouldn't describe her as dreamy, Duchess. She's a very wide-awake little minx with a genius for making trouble."

"I'm sorry to hear that, but don't you think she deserves a treat, after working so hard and landing that scholarship? It so happens that I'll be down your way next weekend, and I hope you'll allow me to take her out to lunch on Sunday, so that I can write to her mother and say I've seen her."

"I'm afraid that's out of the question, Duchess."

"Oh, but why? I don't know what she's done to upset you, but surely in the circumstances—"

"This is not a disciplinary measure, but for her own protection. Last summer an unbalanced woman claim-

ing to be a friend of her parents invited her out to lunch and made a brutal attack on her. I have had to make it a rule for her not to have visitors without a written authorization from her parents."

"Good heavens, what sort of brutal attack? Did she lose a lot of blood?"

"What a strange question. No, but a cut on her arm needed four stitches and she was thrown out of the car in a terrible state miles from here. Perhaps you would like to write to Mrs Derbinsky for permission, and come to see Sandra some other time. Good afternoon, Duchess."

"Lance? Where the hell have you been, I've had you paged in every bar in Wellington. Listen, you're catching the late plane back if you have to ride on an aileron. You've been badly left."

"Why? What gives?"

"Every paper in New Zealand was sent a set of pictures like yours, the Agriculture Department's reaction is on the wire, saying they'll investigate. The can of worms in Kirkstone is wide open, the reign of terror is over, the people who didn't have their fingers in the gravy are informing on the collaborators who did, they'll be shaving women's heads next. I want you back in Kirkstone by dawn tomorrow, so move."

For the next few days the papers were full of the Mount Ephraim scandal. Hidden microphones had been found in all the motel rooms and in a private room at Brown's Hotel, and fraudulently written-off equipment in the homes of almost every employee of the two state farms. Among the victims of the Watson-

Moffat terror, the Harrisons claimed that their wool-shed had been burnt down as a reprisal for having told Ted Murphy that an almost new utility, allegedly a write-off after a crash, had surreptitiously become the property of a hired hand at Mount Shelley. Pilots working for local air taxi firms claimed not to know why charters which involved flying over Mount Ephraim were always refused.

No great intelligence was needed to deduce from the press reports that Rosie had been murdered because she was about to expose these malpractices, and the public was more or less invited to pick her murderer from a short list consisting of Thornhill, Watson, Moffat and Crampton. Thornhill was alleged-ly on holiday in Tasmania and not available for comment. The others were still being interrogated.

Inspector Brent had told the press that the photo-graphs sent anonymously to newspapers merely con-firmed information already in his possession, and that he had been pursuing this line of enquiry for some time. Asked about the role of petite, attractive Celia Grant, who had at one time seemed to be a key figure in the case, he explained that reports of a quarrel between her and Mrs Murphy had been greatly exaggerated. Her presence in Kirkstone at the time of the murder was a coincidence; she had gone there to enquire about a friend of Mrs Murphy's who was believed to be on holiday in New Zealand, and whose family was anxious to contact him.

Being thus reduced to insignificance did not protect Celia from occasional press enquiries. She turned these to advantage to publicize the fact that the "friend believed to be on holiday" whom she was trying to contact was Lord Albert Melton. She hoped vaguely that this might bring in information from members of the public who had had dealings with him, or even shame the Narcotics people into being more communicative. But the next turn of events was, as usual with Bertie, not foreseeable.

"News desk, please."

". . . News desk here."

"I have an announcement to make. A communiqué of the Utu Liberation Army."

"Is this some kind of joke?"

"No. I will give you a code word. Pomegranate. Do you recognize it?"

"Offhand, no."

"You'll find it in the list of codewords used to authenticate announcements connected with the campaign to stop the South African rugby tour."

"Oh, that. I believe we have that list somewhere in the office. Want me to look for it?"

"No. Are you ready to receive the communiqué?"

"Okay, go ahead. What sort of army did you say you are?"

"This is a communiqué of the Utu Liberation Army. In a recent operation our forces took hostage a prominent British public figure, Lord Albert Melton. Conditions for his release are as follows. One. A full-page statement by the Utu Liberation Army will be published in all New Zealand newspapers exposing the injustices inflicted on the Maori people by the unequal Waitangi Treaty of 1840. Two. The annual celebration of the Waitangi Treaty on the sixth of February, which is an insult to the Maori people, is to

159

be abolished. If this condition is not met, the hostage
will be killed on February the sixth next, at a time
coinciding with the holding of the ceremony."

"Hullo?"

"I'm still here. Did you get all that?"

"Yes, but who did you say the prominent British
public figure was?"

"Lord Albert Melton."

"I thought that was what you said, but who's he?"

"A member of the House of Lords and a public
personality. You don't read your own newspaper, he
was in it this morning. 'Believed to be on holiday in
New Zealand,' you said. Not anymore. 'Bye."

"Jim, before I ring Hermione, could it be a hoax?"
Celia asked.

"I don't think so. The code word's a recognized
one, it was used by one of the more extreme groups
involved in the campaign to wreck the South African
rugby tour. Nobody's heard of this Utu Liberation
Army, but that tour fuelled a lot of extremism, it was
the first time that quite a large section of the
population saw the police as the enemy, wearing riot
gear and either 'behaving brutally' or 'standing no
nonsense,' according to your point of view. This so-
called army is probably a tiny group of very determined people who stayed together after the tour ended
and kept their old password."

"Why do they object so to the thing on February the
sixth?" Celia asked.

"It's New Zealand's national day. They celebrate it
at Waitangi, the place where the original treaty was
signed between Queen Victoria's representative and a

group of Maori chiefs on February the sixth 1840. When this arrangement was made no one faced the fact that the Treaty of Waitangi is highly controversial. A lot of the chiefs weren't there and didn't sign it and those who did probably didn't understand what it meant. They certainly didn't understand that if you sold your land you couldn't camp and hunt on it or grow kumara* on it as you'd always done. The man who drew up the treaty was probably quite sincere in thinking it protected the Maoris from exploitation, but the settlers took it as a licence to diddle them out of every bit of land they could.

"For a long time no one bothered much about the fact that February the sixth wasn't really an anniversary to celebrate. Waitangi's a beautiful place, it's usually a lovely summer evening, and they have speeches and a marvellous display of Maori singing and dancing, but the fact is, the harmony between the races has never been as idyllic as the *pakehas* thought it was. The old grievance about land has always been there in the background, and a lot of Maoris didn't see why they should accept the Protestant work-ethic and do well at school and join the *pakeha* rat-race. When the recession came they were the low-paid manual workers who went to the wall and the thing boiled up into a crisis. What these Utu people are saying is, sentiment about racial harmony on Waitangi Day is hypocrisy, and admiration for Maori singing and dancing is no substitute for social justice."

"By which is meant, giving the Maoris back their land."

*A kind of sweet potato.

"I suppose so, but there's a huge rugby stadium somewhere that's supposed to be built on a very *tapu* Maori sight, how can you unscramble the omelette? The point is, these people have hit on a marvellously effective way of highlighting a whole range of social problems. Terrorism is basically theatre, and this is very effective theatre."

"My dear Jim, kidnapping the unspeakable Bertie for political reasons comes under the Theatre of the Absurd."

"Terrorists live in a closed world, they aren't necessarily well informed. They probably think a lord from England must be important."

"Bertie probably told them he was, it would be like him to. He can't have explained that it was only a courtesy title, not a peerage, they talked on the phone about the the House of Lords. Dear me, all this and smuggling too."

"About that, H.E. rang the Narcotics people in Auckland just now and said they'd damn well got to tell him what they knew about the smuggling episode. It turns out that Bertie made the Sydney customs suspicious by flying in and out several times a week, so they searched him and found some kind of body belt which had obviously been used for smuggling. There was nothing in the belt, which puzzled them so they decided to keep it and analyze it for traces of heroin etcetera. But Bertie seems to have told them some fairly convincing story, so they didn't arrest him, they shipped him back to Auckland and told the police there to confiscate his passport pending the results of the analysis. They did, but Bertie only spent one night in the hotel he'd given as his address, then vanished into the blue for good."

"Goodness, when was all this, Jim?"

"Last week. He vanished on the Tuesday, the day you arrived from England."

"If they kidnapped him then, they waited for a week before they issued their communiqué. Why?"

"They were waiting for the outcry to start about the mysterious disappearance of their important public figure. When they saw this morning's papers they realized there wouldn't be an outcry, no one was even sure he was in New Zealand."

"Which reminds me," said Celia. "I must ring Hermione before she hears about it in the morning radio bulletins."

"Kidnapped?" shrieked Hermione. "How typical of Bertie, I can't bear it. When are they due to kill him?"

"On February the sixth."

"That's not for ages! When they do we can sell the Rembrandt without getting his signature, but meanwhile we'll be paying interest on a huge bank loan. Can't they be persuaded to hurry up?"

"Not with decency."

"I know dear, I was only joking, though how I have the heart to joke I can't imagine. Everard and I had better come and cope, Muriel would be hopeless. I'll ring the airline now."

"Hold it, Hermione. The High Commission's in touch with the anti-terrorist people who will be in charge of the negotiations, if any, because kidnapping Bertie counts as terrorism. You'd better wait and see what they advise, it might be a mistake to seem too keen at this stage."

After a lot more argument Hermione was persuaded to stay at home, at least for the present.

Celia went to bed early and slept like a log till three, when she woke in a state of shock, as if after a bad dream. Sitting bolt upright in bed, she managed to remember where she was, and then tried to discover what was wrong with her. She had been disoriented not by a nightmare, but by an all-important idea which had crept up out of her subconscious mind and hit her like a blow on the head from a sledgehammer.

Why hadn't she thought of it before? It was so obvious: Bertie had spent only one night in his Auckland hotel. Next day an oldish passenger with a beard had arrived at Christchurch Airport. *But he was thin*. Once one realized that, everything fell into place and made sense.

It would be mid-afternoon at Melsingham and there was something she must ask Hermione at once. She got out of bed and crept to the telephone.

❧ EIGHT ❧

"You're quite right, Celia dear," said Hermione when she phoned back next morning, "except that he didn't have to go to a theatrical costumier. There was one in Muriel's attic all the time. Her grandmother used to get up amateur theatricals to amuse Edward the Seventh."

"Please be more specific," Celia urged. "What was there one of in Muriel's attic?"

"A cage, dear. That's the proper name for it, a sort of wicker thing that thin actors wear when they have to be Falstaff, wasn't that what you meant? A huge affair, you could smuggle Birnam Wood to Dunsinane in it, which I gather is what Bertie did."

"Are you sure it's gone, Hermione?"

"Absolutely. I'm at Muriel's, I've been in the attic to look. The box is labelled and it's empty."

"Are you sure it was Bertie who took it?"

"Of course, dear, who else would? Where he got

the clothes to go over it is a mystery, one of those outsize places, I suppose, saying it was for amateur theatricals, but you were right about the contact lenses. I phoned his oculist like you said, and yes, he actually managed to fit Bertie with some, though it seems to have been a traumatic experience for all concerned, his trumpetings could be heard at the other end of Wimpole Street, and the oculist says yes, you're right, he was growing a beard. Are you sure I shouldn't jump into the next plane?"

"Don't decide anything till we've talked to the anti-terrorist people here, we're seeing them at ten."

"But Celia dear—"

Jim was hovering with an alarmed look. "I say, Celia—"

"Are you still there, Celia?" Hermione asked.

"One minute Hermione. Jim's trying to tell me something. What is it, Jim?"

"I think Lucy's baby's started to arrive."

"Hermione, did you hear that? I'll have to ring you back. Now, Jim, I'll come and see, but there's no need to look as if Reagan had started a nuclear war. . . . Yes, Hermione, I'll ring you back after we've talked to the anti-terrorist people."

It was clear that Jim was right about the baby. "Ouch!" said Lucy. "This is agony, I've changed my mind, I think I'll adopt one instead."

What was to be done about the appointment with the anti-terrorist authorities? Jim would have to take Lucy to hospital and stay with her till she produced her infant, the virility test for husbands in the labour ward was now compulsory. Did Celia mind keeping the appointment by herself, he asked.

"Not if you brief me. Who do I ask to see?"

"Colonel Forbes of the Special Security Service."

"Which is what?"

"Directly responsible to the Prime Minister and alleged by the left to be very sinister, so I expect it's efficient though you may find the atmosphere a bit spooky. Tell them I'll make contact later, or someone else from the High Commission will."

Having tucked Lucy anxiously into Jim's car, Celia set off by taxi to the Old Government Building. In her worry about Lucy she failed to be impressed by the fact that it was the second largest wooden building in the world and forced herself not to take an irrational dislike to Colonel Forbes, who turned out to be a distinguished greyhead with hawk eyes and a nobly hooked nose. Her apology for Jim's absence was received with a show of carefully controlled impatience which downgraded her to the status of a distraught female out of whom no sense could be got in the absence of a High Commission representative to help keep her in order. Nevertheless, he decided to proceed.

"Is Lord Albert a cool, organized sort of man? The kind who'd react to the situation calmly and try to gain the hostage-takers' confidence?"

"No. He loses his temper and starts to shout on the slightest provocation."

Forbes made a face. "That's bad. Terrorists are hair-trigger people. They frighten easily too. Get them excited and they do silly things like killing their hostages. Now about his family. Are they in a position to pay a large ransom if one is asked for?"

"His wife is very wealthy, I believe."

"The government's determined to prevent a ransom being paid," said Forbes, "for fear of copycat hostage-takings."

"There's another interested party, his nephew the Duke. He has crippling financial problems. To solve the worst of them he needs Lord Albert's signature, or failing that, proof of his death."

"Would you explain that, please?"

Celia did so concisely and added: "The Duchess talks of arriving by the next available plane, to keep in touch with the situation on the spot. What's your advice?"

"Tell her to stay where she is, and say as little as possible to the media."

"I'll try, but she's a very determined woman."

"Give me her number and I'll ring her. The tactic is to play this long, wear them down. Saying nothing can be done till a member of the family arrives is one of the stock ways of stalling. They may contact you, because reports that you're acting for the family have appeared in the press. I'd better tell you exactly what to do if that happens—"

"Thank you. But if I may interrupt, perhaps I should mention at this stage that I think I know who the hostage-takers are."

Forbes' hawk eyes took on a glazed look. "I'm sorry, what was that again?"

"I said, I think I know who the hostage-takers are. One of them's called Bazzer, would that be his surname?"

"No, it's colloquial for 'Barry', there must be several thousand of them in the country."

"This one's in his twenties, blond, blue eyes, height

about five foot nine, handsome in a thin-faced nervy way. He's supposed to be the ringleader, but there's a girl called Jessie who's the real brains behind the thing. She's three-quarters Maori and I'm sure it was her idea to use Lord Albert to publicize Maori grievances and highlight the controversial side of Waitangi Day. There's also Reg and Andy and a red-haired young man whose name I don't know. I could give you detailed descriptions, but to judge from your expression it would be a waste of time, you obviously don't believe me."

Colonel Forbes adjusted his face politely. "Tell me, please, why you suspect these people. Where and when did you come across them?"

"On the day before Mrs Murphy was shot, at a meeting in Kirkstone to protest against the government hydro-electric scheme. I assumed at first that she got them to Kirkstone to swell the volume of protest against the dam, but I was wrong. I was also wrong in assuming that she organized the meeting about the dam to embarrass Trevor Thornhill, whom she hated because he started the rumpus about her husband's intrigue with Sandra Derbinsky, and that the fake rarities planted out in the Kirkstone Valley were part of the same plan.

"But I soon realized that she must be aiming much higher. Making a prominent politician look slightly foolish over a hydro-electric scheme was a feeble sort of revenge for an injury to her husband which was much more serious than the public knew. Because Mr Murphy had his suspicions about corruption at the two state farms and was investigating them, he was led into a honey-trap to discredit him and make him harmless. I won't trouble you with the details of the honey-trap, except that one of its ramifications gave the managers of the two farms a blackmailing hold over Trevor Thornhill, which they used to force him to let them extend their operations and set up a full-scale black market farm on his land. Mrs Murphy's aim was to secure evidence that this farm existed, thereby ruining the three people she held responsible for her husband's death.

"You'll have seen the photos of the farm that appeared in the press. I was astonished that so many of the papers missed an obvious point about those photos, namely when they were taken. In the aerial views the trees are bare. They were taken in winter, July or August at the latest."

"That's right," said Forbes. "There was a report in this morning's papers, a Dunedin survey firm says Mrs Murphy commissioned them and they were taken in August, while she was in the UK."

"But the air photos didn't prove how criminal the whole operation was," Celia went on. "Someone had to go in on the ground and record a lot of detail, serial numbers on equipment and so on. If you look at the photos taken at ground level, you'll find that the trees in the background are in full leaf, and there's even something that looks like a dandelion between the front feet of a very impressive bull. They were taken much later, in December, say.

"Smuggling a photographic team in to take those pictures was quite a problem, because Moffat and Watson have built up defences in depth to keep people out of the sensitive area. There are even hidden microphones in the rooms at places where strangers are liable to stay. Mrs Murphy solved the problem brilliantly. She filled the township with botanists and pressmen and people who are opposed to dams on principle, and installed the phoney rarities so that they all came surging up the valley to see them, and the crowd swamped the Moffat-Watson surveillance system and made it possible to get a photographic team into the Mount Ephraim forest and right up to the farm. The team consisted of Bazzer, Jessie, Andy, Reg and the red-haired young man whose name I don't know."

"This is fine," Forbes interrupted. "But how d'you know it was them that took the pictures?"

"Partly for a reason I'll explain in a moment, and partly because after the meeting in the woolshed they all disappeared during the night complete with the van they'd driven down from Auckland in. Everyone assumed that they'd gone back there, but I don't think they did. During the night they drove up to the Kirkstone Valley and got into the Mount Ephraim forest through a well-camouflaged Taranaki gate on to a track which isn't marked on any map though it showed up on the air photos that Mrs Murphy had given them to guide them to the target area. I imagine they hid the van under the trees somewhere and made a stealthy approach on foot. They took the pictures while the stock-hand was still asleep or milking or feeding cattle in an outlying paddock, then they lay up till nightfall so that they wouldn't be seen on their way down the valley; because if Moffat and Watson discovered that the place had been raided, they'd arrange for the evidence to disappear before the police moved in."

Forbes had begun to fidget. "This is all very interesting and well-reasoned, Mrs Grant, but how does it connect up with the hostage-taking problem we're supposed to be discussing?"

"Because as Bazzer and company were driving down the Kirkstone Valley to the township, they overtook an elderly gentleman called Lord Albert Melton trudging along on foot, and gave him a lift."

Forbes shrugged, though the movement looked to Celia more like a dignified burp of distaste at being confronted with such an indigestible mass of conjecture. "What on earth was he doing there?"

"That's a long story, which begins earlier this year in England. Mrs Murphy, who was there for another purpose, cultivated his friendship, to put it charitably, in the hope of persuading him to provide her with the spurious rarities she wanted to plant out in the Kirkstone Valley. This wasn't possible for practical reasons and when Mrs Murphy discovered this she went off in a huff. But Lord Albert's enthusiasm for redheads hasn't cooled with age, and when he learnt that a specialist grower of alpines in Australia had died, he came rushing across the world to buy specimens from the widow, smuggle them into New Zealand and plant them out in the Kirkstone Valley, thereby reinstating himself in Mrs Murphy's favour.

"Lord Albert is a skilled grower of cultivated alpines, but he's not strong on plant ecology. I think I realized that his 'rarities' wouldn't deceive experts for very long, so he took elaborate precautions against detection. He's been to New Zealand several times before and is known to the botanical fraternity here. If it was known that he'd spent a lot of time in the Kirkstone area shortly before the 'rarities' were discovered, people would ask why he hadn't discovered them. Why had he crept away and left them to be found by a young and inexperienced botany graduate?

"To avoid being asked such embarrassing questions, he decided to come in disguise. He grew a beard and had contact lenses fitted instead of his usual thick glasses and provided himself with a theatrical 'cage' which served two purposes: nobody could be more incognito than a six-foot beanpole of a man who has suddenly become a mountain of fat, and the cage was roomy enough to hold consignments of plants that had to be smuggled in past the Agriculture Department watchdogs.

"To get a large collection of alpine plants into the country and down to Kirkstone in good condition, he had to make several journeys. Eventually his appearance must have struck the Australian customs as odd, so they searched him. This was two days before the rarities were due to be unveiled by Mrs Murphy in Kirkstone, and I think he was on his way out of the country for good. He had to travel complete with beard and contact lenses to look like his passport photo (he got a new passport, by the way, shortly before he left England). Of course the photo was only head and shoulders, but after going through the Australian customs rather often looking fat he didn't dare show himself there looking thin. So he was wearing his cage, though of course it was empty, as it always was on the outward journey to Australia. If it hadn't been described in the version that reached me as a 'body belt' I'd have realized the truth much earlier.

"So poor Lord Albert was in a frightful fix. His passport had been confiscated and so had an essential bit of his disguise, and you can't even cash traveller's cheques without your passport, so he may have been short of ready money. Mrs Murphy was the only person he could confide in and look to for help, so he flew down to Christchurch and made a beeline for Kirkstone. I don't think he was at all welcome there. He's a very tiresome man, and it's clear from what Mrs Murphy said to me about him that she'd been delighted to see what she thought was the last of him. She may have had trouble getting rid of him before the meeting at which his handiwork was to be unveiled, and I'm sure she was horrified to see him back.

"What on earth was she to do with him? He was known there as 'Stanley Parker', the whole township would be agog with curiosity when it saw that her mysterious house guest had lost six or seven stone in less than a week. How could she explain him to the huge influx of pressmen and botanists that she was expecting at any moment? She decided to hide him. Inspector Brent at Kirkstone will confirm that traces of the camp that she improvised for 'Parker' were found in the bush near the lower boundary of the Mount Ephraim sheep run.

"Next day she was too busy with the preparations for the meeting to do much about him. But as soon as she could she went up to Mount Ephraim to discuss what was to happen to him next. The discussion never took place because she was shot. When she didn't turn up Lord Albert explored and found her body. Now

174

what was he to do? If he stayed and told the fantastic and very embarrassing truth about his reasons for being where he was nobody would believe him, so he decided to slip away. But the gorge between him and the township was teeming with sightseers, so he had to hide up till after dark before he made a move.

"And now at last I have answered your question. This is why Lord Albert Melton was trudging down the Kirkstone Valley towards the township in the dark when a van containing the Utu Liberation Army overtook him and gave him a lift.

"When he discovered that they weren't local people and were going straight back to Auckland, he leapt at what looked like a marvellous chance to get clear of the area and no questions asked. Goodness knows what he told them to account for him being where he was. It must have been something pretty fancy that made him seem very important, which was silly of him. If he'd pretended to be a tramp or something they wouldn't have kidnapped him."

There was a long silence while Forbes weighed up what she had said. His hawk eyes looked straight through Celia, who began to suspect that he was trying to convince himself that she wasn't there. When at last he spoke, his verdict was a surprise. "I congratulate you on a remarkably coherent piece of reasoning, Mrs Grant. Please don't misunderstand me or think I'm not taking you seriously if I point out that all we have here is an elaborate but unproven theory."

"Oh, I agree. But there are some things you could check. Was what the Australian customs found a body belt or something much bigger? Has Lord Albert got a beard and no glasses in the photo on his new passport?

The Auckland police confiscated it, you could check that by phone. It would be interesting to make the kidnappers produce a photograph of him holding an up-to-date newspaper. That's often done to prove that the hostage is still alive. Then we'd know if he has a Parker-style beard or not."

He drummed with his fingers on the desk, thinking. Then he stood up. "Wait here for a moment, d'you mind?"

The "moment" proved very long and Celia began to fidget. Concentrating for so long on Bertie and his problems had been quite an effort, she had had to force herself not to worry about Lucy. According to her doctor everything was supposed to be quite normal, but from what Celia remembered of her own struggles to produce her children, obstetricians were capable of stretching the word "normal" to cover some pretty hectic goings-on. What was happening? She was looking in the phone book for the hospital's number when Forbes came back into the room.

"You're right, he has a beard in his passport picture and no glasses," he reported, "and the so-called body belt was a huge wicker affair, they'd never seen anything like it. I checked with Inspector Brent in Kirkstone, and he confirms that traces of a camp were found about a mile from the scene of the murder." Without any change of tone he added: "Brent raised a point that I have to check with you. He thinks you shot Mrs Murphy."

"Really? I thought he'd forgotten that nonsense."

"His suspicions were revived when I told him that 'Parker' was an *alias* for Lord Albert Melton, whose trail you admitted having followed to Kirkstone. He thinks you killed her out of jealousy, because Lord Albert was your former lover and she'd stolen him from you."

"How extraordinary that a man with the physique of a muscle-bound chorus boy should have a romantic fiction mind."

"Something must have given him the idea."

"Yes. Thornhill had an obvious motive for killing Mrs Murphy, and it seemed advisable to take the heat off him somehow. So a hired hand from Mount Shelley was briefed to give Brent a vivid eyewitness description of me at Christchurch airport pleading in vain with my enormously fat lover to return to me. The trouble is, there was no enormously fat lover there for me to plead with, only a much-shrunken, panic-stricken Lord Albert, who came off the plane before mine and shot off to Kirkstone as fast as he could. Did Brent explain to you how I was supposed to have got hold of the gun?"

"He says there was some controversy about when it went missing."

"Yes, that was another attempt by Moffat and Watson to take the heat off Thornhill. Quite unnecessary, I suppose he denied it and they didn't believe him, but he was telling the truth. Which leads me to mention an obvious fact that occurred to me a few moments ago. Mrs Murphy was shot by Lord Albert."

Forbes choked back what sounded like a controlled explosion of laughter. "Please don't say things like that without warning, it unnerves me. You must be joking."

"No. I'm sorry, I should have though of it earlier, but things have been happening rather fast and I've been worried about my daughter, who's having a baby. Why do I know he shot her, let me think. Oh yes, we know from the traces of his camp that he shot and cooked a bird, so he must have had a gun. *The* gun in fact, the one that was stolen from the men who were repairing the fence. I don't think he meant to steal it. He saw it lying there in their utility and they were working quite a distance away and wouldn't be back for some time. Being Lord Albert he saw no reason why he shouldn't borrow it and shoot something to supplement the perhaps rather meagre rations which a very bad-tempered Mrs Murphy had provided.

"But presently the utility was driven away, because the feckless fence-repairers hadn't enough wire with them and had to drive down to the township to get more. When Lord Albert went back to return the gun there was no utility. So he hung on to it, and next day it turns up wiped clean of fingerprints beside Mrs Murphy's body."

"Why would he want to shoot her, though? He was relying on her to get him out of his scrape, she's the last person he'd want dead, he had no motive."

"If you're Lord Albert Melton with a gun in your hand, you don't need a motive, that was one of the first things the Duchess told me about him. When he turned out for the shoot at Melsingham his appearance was the signal for a general panic, he's half blind and frightfully dangerous and looses off more or less at random. That's what happened."

"You're not saying he killed her by accident?"

"Yes. He'd shot a bird for the pot the previous day and he was out with the gun looking for another. I've been to the spot, it's on a narrow winding path through thick bush and he was probably being stealthy, hiding behind trees and so on. I'd been following Mrs Murphy and she'd dodged about to shake me off, so he wasn't expecting her to arrive from that direction. He saw something move on the other side of a bush and blazed away at it with both barrels, and that was that."

Forbes had looked grim before. Now he looked even grimmer. "Are you sure about this?"

"Yes. If he didn't take the gun, how did he manage to shoot the bird he cooked? What happened to the photographs that Mrs Murphy grabbed from me and took into the Mount Ephaim forest? The police didn't find them on the body, and the only person with a motive for not leaving them there to be found was Lord Albert."

"I'm sure you realize what's worrying me," said Forbes.

"Of course: how will the kidnappers react if they realize that their reactionary aristocrat of a hostage is also the killer of Red Rosie, the idol of the left? One worries especially about Bazzer, who had what he probably thinks of as a love affair with her."

"What's your guess? They picked him up a few miles from where she was shot, don't they suspect him?"

"They didn't when they picked him up and gave him a lift, I'm sure of that. Remember, no one knew that night that Mrs Murphy was dead, she wasn't found till the next morning, so they probably believed whatever account he gave of himself, and decided on the basis of it that he was worth holding as a hostage. Later, when they heard that Mrs Murphy had been shot, what's appeared in the press may have given them other ideas. Do they know his camp's been found?''

"I've seen nothing about it in the press."

"In that case they've no reason to suppose that he's ever been near where she was shot. What they believe depends very much on what he's told them."

"Hi, Bertie."

"Hi, you nauseating little pipsqueak."

"Here's your dinner. You want it?"

"No, but I'd better have it. All food in this underdeveloped country is uneatable, but what you're giving me would make a camel vomit."

"It's all you'll get."

"Not being able to see it makes it worse. Why can't you unblindfold me and give me back my contact lenses?"

"Because you're not co-operating with us, Bertie. You tell us lies. There's a profile of you in today's papers, you're not a proper lord with a seat in parliament, you're only called that because you're a duke's younger brother."

"I never said I was a peer. You and your fellow-ignoramuses decided I was one, and I couldn't be bothered to undeceive you."

"The more I hear from you, the less I believe."

"That's your problem. You have to decide whether I'm telling the truth or adopting a series of ruses to confuse you representatives of the unwashed proletariat. I can only tell you that I have a strict regard for the truth."

"Your regard for the truth reminds me of the late Adolf Hitler's."

"Don't bring him into it, for God's sake. Dis-

appointing little shit, if he'd been more of a gent and less of a gangster he'd have made a superb ruler for a united Europe.''

"Careful, Bertie. That line of talk's making my trigger finger very itchy.''

"You won't shoot me, you haven't got the guts.''

"Listen, hostages are supposed to fall abjectly in love with their kidnappers, why can't you do that and pipe down?''

"A homosexual orgy would relieve the boredom, but I'd rather have the girl. Or is she as black as a boot, she sounds like it.''

". . . .''

"Ow. That hurt.''

"It was meant to. Let's go through the whole damn story again and see if we can make sense of it. What were you doing up there on Mount Ephraim?''

"Collecting black stilts' eggs, which is illegal. That's why I had to slink away from the area under cover of night.''

"What a load of balls. Black stilts are more or less extinct and you didn't have any eggs.''

"I know that, you fool, it was only my cover story. I was employed by the CIA to investigate reports of a secret Russian tracking station up on Mount Ephraim.''

"Go on.''

"Must I go through it all again? Oh, very well. I found what they thought was the tracking station, and it was only where someone was doing a spot of black market farming. Trust the CIA to get it wrong, they always do.''

"I'm not even sure you're Lord Albert Melton. The photo of him in the papers has glasses and no beard.''

"I'm in disguise, you fool. You can't spy for the CIA without a false nose or something."

"Who's Celia Grant who came to Kirkstone looking for you?"

"Another CIA operative making contact, they hadn't heard from me for weeks and wondered where I was."

"She says she went to Kirkstone to get your address from Rose Murphy, because Rosie's a friend of yours."

"What of it? Operative Grant had to have a cover story, you can't say 'I'm here on behalf of the CIA to look for one of our men who hasn't reported in lately'."

"That's not funny, damn you. There's some tie-up between you and Rose Murphy and this Mrs Grant, and Rosie has been murdered. I want to know what the tie-up is, because I think one or other of you killed her. In thirty seconds from now I shall start hitting you, and I shall go on hitting you till I'm told the truth."

"I'd like you to come to Auckland with me," said Forbes. "There's a plane at one."

"No. Not possible. Sorry."

"Please. That's the hostage-takers' base. You've met them and you know more about the hostage than anyone else. We need you there on the spot."

"No, really, all the time we've been talking I've had acute split-mind symptoms, worrying about something quite different, I hope I didn't sound like an escaped mental patient. My daughter's having her first baby, she went into labour this morning."

"Oh yes, you told me, that's why your son-in-law couldn't come," said Forbes, lifting the telephone. "Which hospital?"

Celia told him. "Her name's Mrs Blakewell."

He told a secretary to phone the hospital, then stood staring out of the window. "I wish we knew whether they suspect Lord Albert of shooting Mrs Murphy."

Celia forced her mind back to Bertie and his problems. "Can't you get the media to mislead them a bit?"

"They'll co-operate if I ask them not to publish certain things, for instance the fact that traces of a camp made by a suspect were found near the scene of the crime. It will help if the hostage-takers don't know that, but we can't ask the media to publish anything misleading."

"Why not? Inspector Brent has been dishing out misleading information to them for days."

"But he believed it," Forbes objected.

"Can't he be persuaded to go on misleading himself publicly, like a dog chasing its tail? Phone him and say the Grant woman's acting suspiciously and he's probably right, she did murder her dreadful fat lover after all. Go on, I don't mind."

"It's kind of you to offer, Mrs Grant, but he's already changed his mind publicly about you once, and we don't want to make him look even more of a fool. From what I gather he's concentrating on building up a case against Thornhill. If we let matters take their course, quite a lot of that will filter through into the media."

A secretary came into the room, and read out from

her note pad: "Mrs Blakewell gave birth to a son twenty minutes ago. Both are doing well."

Forbes got his congratulations over with almost indecent haste. "Now, Mrs Grant. I'll order a car for you and you can go home and pack, then call in at the hospital on your way to the airport to see your daughter and the baby, and catch the two o'clock flight to Auckland. How about it?"

Celia, who had been wondering how much the baby weighed, collected her wits. "Oh dear, I suppose I must."

Thirty hectic minutes later she had packed a bag and was leaping out of the police car at the maternity entrance to the hospital. She was determined to see Lucy before she left for Auckland, even if it meant missing the plane. The ward sister, entrenched behind a fathers-only rule, treated her like a hysterical old fusspot who had to be dealt with firmly, but Jim, looking exhausted but grinning broadly, took charge and persuaded higher authority to relax the ban.

"Mrs Blakewell will see you now," said the ward sister with an I-hope-you're-satisfied intonation, "but you won't get much out of her, she's very exhausted."

Lucy greeted her with an excited but confused burble, in which the main ingredient seemed to be relief that the baby had the right number of limbs and even, astonishingly, a complete set of fingernails. Celia had intended to explain to her why she had to desert her post and rush off to Auckland, but Lucy was in no state to take the information in. The ward sister was right, it was idiotic of her to make such a fuss and to top everything, she went weepy at the sight of the baby. How ridiculous, she thought, a new-born baby is a hideous object like a boiled monkey, I must pull myself together. But why did this one make her think of Roger and miss him dreadfully?

Thanks to a screaming police siren she caught the Auckland plane with minutes to spare. As she climbed into it she remembered guiltily that she had promised to ring Hermione back. Nothing could be done about that in an aircraft flying at whatever-it-was thousand feet, and anyway it was in the middle of the night in England. Hermione was very strong-willed, could she be dissuaded from arriving post haste and ordering the anti-terrorist squad about? And what about the time-table, how long would the business in Auckland take and would it be over before Lucy was discharged from hospital? Celia was still worrying about all this when the no-smoking light came on for the landing at Auckland, New Zealand's largest city.

Seen from the air Auckland was a vast suburban sprawl of boxlike little houses on quarter-acre plots, which had spread like some plant disease over an intricately beautiful scene of bays and headlands and sheltered harbours. The little houses stretched as far as the eye could see, surely there must be a centre somewhere? Yes, there it was, a tiny group of high-rise buildings down by the steamer piers of the main waterfront. Somewhere in all this was Bertie, watched over by masked gunmen. How on earth was he to be found?

A police car was waiting to take her into town. The driver pointed out landmarks, but it was the non-landmarks that impressed her. The houses were very close together and wooden, how soundproof were they? Bertie in captivity would bellow with rage, they would have to gag him.

According to the driver some of the suburbs they passed through were good residential aras. Others inhabited largely by the under-privileged, Maoris and Polynesian immigrants from the islands, were "rough". Celia could detect no difference between the two, having failed to grasp that in a subtropical climate where agapanthus grew like a weed, a gardenful of tibouchinas and alamanders and hibiscus was no guarantee of respectability. The suburban shopping centres had a frontier-town look, with concrete boardwalks along the fronts of the shops, as if cowboys might clatter down the street and tie up their horses to the posts. Some of the men had dressed the part as pioneers of empire, with their knees showing between strangely long shorts and their stocking tops.

Colonel Forbes had caught an earlier plane, and was waiting for her at an ornate Victorian-style wooden villa with an atmosphere inside which gave her the creeps. It was clearly a New Zealand version of the discreet "safe houses" dear to spy fiction, and accommodated police activities of the sort best not thought about. Forbes produced from a filing cabinet a huge pile of police photos of disgruntled-looking alleged subversives, male and female. She worked through them conscientiously for an hour. None of them looked at all like Bazzer or Jessie or Reg or Andy, or the young man with red hair.

"In that case I'll ask you to look at a film," said Forbes, and settled her down in a small projection theatre with instructions to shout "stop" to the projectionist if she saw anyone she recognized.

She had expected undercover footage taken with

hidden police cameras. What she saw was a feature-length documentary called "Patu", made by a Maori director. It told the story of a mass agitation against a South African rugby tour of New Zealand, tracing the course of events from huge but peaceful demonstrations before the tour and during the early matches, through scenes of escalating violence, with police in riot gear confronting crowds determined to disrupt matches and ensure that no rugby team from sport-segregated South Africa ever toured New Zealand again.

She watched the film in a state of moral confusion. Her sympathies were with the demonstrators and she was shocked to find herself seeing it for a purpose for which it was not intended under the auspices of a somewhat louche secret police organization. But Bertie's kidnappers had to be identified somehow, and Bazzer and company would certainly have opposed the tour. As she tried to convince herself that the end justified the means, the film came to one of its moments of triumphant climax. The protesters had broken through barbed wire defences laid by the army and through a police cordon and had surged into the stadium. Several hundred of them were massed in the middle of the pitch, bringing the match to a halt. Most of them wore motorcycling helmets as a protection against the police truncheons.

"Stop!" Celia called.

"Right, now I'll show it you frame by frame," said the projectionist. "Tell me when I get to the right one."

"Now," said Celia.

There, standing close together in the foreground of the picture, were Bazzer and Jessie.

* * *

"Haere mai, Jessie."

"Hi, Bazzer."

"How is he? Has he said anything more?"

"No."

"Then why the hell didn't you make him? I want to know."

"Why? Who cares whether he killed Rosie or not?"

"I do, Jessie."

"Just because Rosie let you shag with her twice? Be your age, if Bertie did kill her there's no political mileage in it. Look at today's papers. The police suspect Thornhill, it stands out a mile. We get much better value out of a National Party MP tried for murder."

"I have to know, Jessie."

"Okay, but don't you dare start knocking him about again. We have to produce him in good shape if the government gives way over Waitangi Day."

"They won't. Why don't we kill him now, save ourselves a lot of bother?"

"Because this is a serious political operation, not an ego-trip for forlorn lovers. Go on in, it's time you relieved Reg."

"What do I do about Christmas?" Celia asked her son-in-law. "Lucy will be back from hospital with the baby, we ought to celebrate, but turkey and a plum-pudding would be madness in this heat."

"Salmon mayonnaise and fruit salad at a beach," Jim prescribed, "under a puhutukawa."

"Which is a Maori beach umbrella made of rushes, or what?"

"A tree covered with scarlet blossom, you must have seen them all along the coast. They're called Christmas trees because that's when they flower."

Celia decided privately that puhutukawa or no puhutukawa, this was not on. Small babies loathed beach picnics and the logistics would be frightful, but she would leave it to Lucy to veto the idea.

Colonel Forbes had called twice to report progress. Armed with stills from the rugby tour film, enlarged to show a close-up of Bazzer, a small army of detectives had established by patient enquiry that his surname was Wilson and that he was the son of divorced parents, neither of whom had been in contact with him for several years. He had dropped out of university after a brillant start and had joined a commune in south Auckland which lived on leisurely car panel-beating, supplemented by discreet drug-peddling. But the commune had melted away at the first sign that the police were interested in it. There was rumoured to be a link with a sister commune which grew marijuana in a remote clearing on the Coromandel Peninsula, but the reports did not say exactly where it was. Despite laborious leg-work, no clue to Jessie's identity had been found.

Hermione had finally faced the fact that she would achieve nothing useful by spending money she could ill afford on the fare to New Zealand, and had not even telephoned for several days. But when the phone woke Celia from her first sleep at one in the morning, she knew at once who the caller would be.

"Celia dear, disaster."

"What sort of disaster, Hermione?"

"I'm sorry, it must be an ungodly hour at your end,

189

but I had to tell you at once. Muriel, heeding the call of wifely duty, is even now hurtling through the first-class air towards you."

"Heavens. What does she propose to do when she gets here?"

"She has all her jewellery with her, including a diamond necklace the size of a horse-collar, and intends to ransom Bertie with it."

"But nobody's *asked* for a ransom."

"I know, dear, but Muriel's a very conventional woman. I don't think she even likes Bertie much, but she's determined to be seen to do the right thing."

"When's she due? What's the flight number?"

"I don't know, she slunk off furtively because she knew I'd disapprove."

"Horrors, if she starts hawking her baubles around in the Auckland subculture she'll be robbed and probably killed. Even if it is the middle of the night, I think I'll ring my tame anti-terrorist, he can probably get it all confiscated under some customs regulation."

"You do that, dear. I'll hang up."

Christmas came and went. The baby wailed systematically from two to four every afternoon, which seemed to be its chosen way of taking exercise, but was otherwise docile. Moffat and Watson had been arrested for "theft as a servant"—embezzlement. Their application for bail was refused, to cure them temporarily of their habit of intimidating witnesses. Thornhill had returned from Tasmania spluttering with synthetic indignation. He had no idea, he said, that the two farm managers had established what he called a "thieves' kitchen" on his property. Nobody believed this, but everyone wondered why he had lent himself to such a squalid piece of low-level corruption. Inspector Brent had at last grasped that Thornhill had a strong motive for murdering Rosie. To discourage him from arresting Thornhill on a murder charge, Colonel Forbes had thought it only fair to alert him to the case against another strong suspect. Brent retorted that not even a pommy lord could be as careless as that with a gun, and had continued to throw out dark hints that the Ted Murphy sex scandal had been a frame-up by Thornhill.

In January the police found and raided the marijuana farm on the Coromandel Peninsula which was supposed to have links with Bazzer's car-repairing commune in Auckland. Bertie was not being held there, and interrogation of the sullen inhabitants yielded nothing relevant. They were all held on drug charges and photographed. The resulting rogues' gallery of far-from-innocent young faces were shown to Celia, but Jessie, Andy, Reg and the red-haired young man were not among them.

On Forbes' advice Celia had had no contact with Muriel Melton apart from one brief phone call, but knowing what she was up to posed no problem. Her lamentations when the Prime Minister refused to relent or cancel the Waitangi Day ceremony, or even to see her, were fully reported in the papers and on television. Early in the New Year she removed herself to Auckland, the supposed scene of her husband's incarceration, and settled down to await developments in a suite in a waterfront luxury hotel. Her pleas to his captors produced one meagre result. The *New Zealand Herald* received through the post a photo of him holding a recent issue of that paper. He was clean shaven and wearing glasses. Presumably he had been tidied up to resemble photos of him in his normal guise which had appeared in the press. Muriel's exclamations of gratitude for this evidence that her husband was still alive, and her hopes for his future deliverance, filled half a column in the *Herald*.

Celia was less hopeful.

"We'll get a break soon," Forbes assured her. "We're due for a bit of luck."

But the luck, when it came, was bad. Thornhill, tiring of Inspector Brent's insinuations and hints, complained publicly that a whispering campaign against him was being fostered by the extreme left, and that the inexcusable delay in holding the inquest on Rose Murphy was allowing rumours to circulate which were damaging to innocent parties. It was nonsense to say that more time was needed to collect evidence, there was plenty of that already. It was well known, for instance, that traces of a camp had been found near the scene of the crime, including evidence that the camper had a shotgun.

"And he said it live on television before they could stop him," said Forbes gloomily.

"You saw it too, Jessie? And the interviewer trying to shush him before he said it? Don't you see, there's been a news blackout on that camp all these weeks, and I know why."

"So do we all, Bazzer, must you bore the pants off us about this? It was Bertie's camp and they think we'll be harder on him if we know he killed Rosie, but what the hell does it matter, he'll be dead in a fortnight anyway."

"Not if they give way and cancel the Waitangi Festival of Interracial Pseudo-Erotica."

"Ha ha, Bazzer, not likely."

"It's a theoretical possibility. If we have to hand him over alive, we hand him over with a written and signed confession, saying how and why he killed Rosie, and this confession I shall now obtain."

"No, Bazzer, you hate his guts, you might kill him. Reg and I will question him if you insist, but first there's something else to decide. Seen yesterday's Herald?"

"About how mad Mrs Bertie wants us to phone her? Use your marbles, Jessie, it's a police trap. Must be, the arsehole press is giving her a big show, she must be playing their game."

"I'm not so sure, she sounds too moronic to play anyone's game. All that wailing about her poor martyred Bertie, and why won't they cancel Waitangi. I'd say she's an embarrassment to the government, making them look flint-hearted and highlighting our campaign against the Treaty."

"Are you saying we should ring her and find out what's on her mind?"

"I did. Yesterday."

"And what was?"

"Hard to say, talking to a real live terrorist got her very overwrought and she forgot what she meant to say. It was all written on bits of paper that she kept losing and most of it didn't make sense."

"Some of it must have done, Jessie."

"Well, there was a lot about us being merciless and wouldn't we soften our hearts and accept a ransom, so

I said it was the government and not us that was merciless and no, we didn't want a ransom, and there was a lot of lamentation about that. Then she said how was he and she was worried because he looked very pale and thin in the picture we sent to the paper, and she was sure the spectacles he was wearing weren't his, he was always losing them and could he see through the ones we'd given him? She'd brought a spare pair with her from England just in case, and also his bible and a box of some cigars he specially liked, and would we let him have them to comfort his last days on earth, and how could she get them to us?"

"My God, Jessie, this is the corniest police trap I ever heard of."

"No one could act as crazy as that unless they really were, but yes, I suppose it must be a trap, the police pick us up when we go to the drop to collect the little parcel of goodies that we've told her to leave there. But I told her the Command Council of the Utu Liberation Army would consider her request and let her know, because I've had an idea. A trap can work two ways. I think we can fix something to give the forces of law and order a great big surprise."

Lady Albert Melton was bewildered, exhausted and very frightened. Since leaving her luxurious hotel suite looking out over the harbour she had been criss-crossing the vast sprawl of Auckland for almost two hours. Bertie's kidnappers had told her to take a taxi to the Auckland Hilton and wait in the lounge till she was contacted.

For 20 minutes nothing happened except being

stared at, which she hated, by people who recognized her from the television news and wondered what on earth she was doing sitting there without a drink or even a book to pass the time. Then she was paged for a phone call and told to go through the same rigmarole at another hotel out near the airport, which proved hard to find. From there she was told to go back to the waterfront and take the ferry across the harbour to Devonport. This she was now doing. No doubt the idea was to make sure the police were not shadowing her, but it was very tiresome. It was long past her dinner time. A stiff breeze was rippling the dark water and she was cold in her thin summer dress. Watching the lights of Auckland recede, she wished most heartily that she had not thought it her duty to embark on this adventure.

She walked ashore at Devonport in a crowd of passengers who fanned out in all directions from the landward end of the pier. Turn right, she had been told, the litter bin beside the third seat along the front. She found it, took the parcel out of the shopping bag she had been carrying all evening. Looking guiltily round, she dropped it in the bin.

There were various people about, but no one was taking any interest in her. Vaguely disappointed by this, she walked back to the pier. The ferry was waiting. She went on board. Presently it started back towards the bright lights of Auckland.

When it reached the other side she decided to walk. Her hotel was only a few hundred yards from the ferry terminal. So far, nothing untoward had happened, and in a few minutes she would be safely back in the hotel lobby.

She had been terrified all evening, but when the attack came it was a complete surprise. A car drew up at the kerb with its engine running. Two men lurched out of it and grabbed her, trying to pull her into the car. But the plainclothes policemen who had been following her radio bleep all evening were quick to close in.

"Well done, Lady Albert," said Forbes as the two kidnappers were being handcuffed. "Well done, everyone."

The driver of the getaway car had abandoned it and melted away into the crowd. The two captured kidnappers refused to make any statement or answer any questions. Celia, flown up next day from Wellington to identify them at Colonel Forbes' sinister Victorian villa, pronounced one to be Reg, and the other to be the red-haired youth whose name she did not know.

"It was a beautifully baited trap, I do congratulate you," she said to Forbes, "and how marvellous that they fell for it."

"They spotted the wrong trap, of course. They thought we'd be watching the drop to see who collected the parcel. They didn't expect us to be watching Lady Albert."

"Why were you so sure they'd try to kidnap her?"

"Simple. As a hostage Lord Albert's all very well in his way, but he's a bit lightweight when it comes to getting our National Day celebrations cancelled. I was sure they'd snatch a few more to build up the pressure. She had publicity value and we set her up to look like a soft target, and they fell for it. There's a fortnight to go, they'll try again, so we're stepping up security on all the likely public figures. I'm sure we'll have a wave of kidnappings before we're through."

"Muriel acted up marvellously," said Celia. "All that half-witted nonsense she talked on television."

"You're too right, when I put it to her she said: 'Well Colonel Forbes, I don't mind how much of a fool I look in public if it will help you to find Bertie.'"

Before Celia went back to Wellington she called at the hotel to congratulate Muriel, whom she found enjoying a sumptuous afternoon tea. "I steered clear of you before, because I didn't want to queer your pitch," she explained. "You were marvellous.

"You see, I thought I owed it to Bertie. He's so helpless, someone has to look after him, and though he's not a very good husband he is my responsibility. So I thought I ought to come here and see if I could do anything."

"Is it true that you brought all your jewellery with you to ransom him with?"

Muriel winked. "I suppose Hermione told you that. No, only the paste copy of my diamond necklace. I didn't know what the situation was here and thought it might come in useful. Did Hermione give you the impression that I'm a moron?"

"To be honest, yes."

"I encourage her to think that, or she'd never leave me alone, she's a ruthless organizer. I'm only eight miles away, and she'd have me selling entrance tickets for that awful house of hers in no time if I wasn't careful. My grandfather pulled ours down, thank God, and rebuilt it in hideous Victorian brick, so I don't have to bother."

Back in Wellington Celia was dropped in on from time to time by Colonel Forbes, to give her progress reports and show her photos of suspected terrorists. The two captured kidnappers still refused to say anything, but Reg had been identified as the youngest son of a very prosperous farmer from the Hamilton area, and his red-haired companion came from a family owning a modest suburban grocery chain. They had met at Wellington University and Forbes had thought it worth assembling a gallery of photographs of their student friends and associates. None of them rang a bell with Celia.

The flat in Wellington was stiflingly hot and the baby was fractious, but Jim was on the skeleton staff holding the fort over the holidays at the High Commission and could not get away. Muriel had acted on an obscure and surely somewhat morbid impulse concerning where she ought to be as the fatal hour for Bertie approached, and had rented a holiday cottage on the Bay of Islands opposite Waitangi. But she was plunged in gloom there and begged Celia to join her. With a little diplomacy Celia got the invitation extended to include Lucy and the baby.

Meanwhile Forbes called again to report a break-through. The Utu Liberation Army had photographed the farm on Mount Ephraim and sent a dozen professionally finished enlargements of the pictures to every newspaper and TV station in the country. No photographic processing firm remembered an order of that size and description. Therefore someone in the group had access to processing equipment. Armed with photos of Reg, Bazzer, Jessie and the red-haired youth, detectives visited every likely firm and asked if any of the three had ever been employed there. They struck lucky with a small firm in one of the sprawling southern suburbs, which recognized Reg's photo. He had been employed there till he vanished without explanation in mid-December.

The home address he had given proved to be a sordid bungalow on a leg-in section* overlooking the southern motorway. It was inhabited by three men and two girls who had moved in a month ago and had never seen the previous tenants, but the neighbours recognized photos of Bazzer, Reg and the red-haired youth. There was also a girl, they said, and her description made it almost certain that she was Jessie. Three other men either lived in the bungalow or visited it regularly. One of them corresponded to Celia's description of Andy, the other two were mysteries.

Here the trail ended for the time being. The whole lot had moved out abruptly in mid-December.

But on the day before Celia left for the Bay of Islands, Forbes called again, exuding a discreet, hawk-eyed satisfaction. Andy had cashed a cheque with a local shopkeeper. It provided him with a surname, a bank account and the home address of his family in Remuera, a suburb so "swept up" and select that the rest of Auckland considered it an uproarious joke. The stroke of luck did not end there. When confronted with the descriptions of the two still unidentified frequenters of the bungalow, Andy's parents recognized them at once as the vicious associates who had led their Andy astray; spoilt boys from families with too much money on whom doting parents had

*A housing plot behind a house facing the street which has sold off its back garden.

lavished boats, cars, holidays abroad—in fact, everything a boy could want. What was wrong with the modern generation? They had no morals and no guts.

"We have five of their names now, Mrs Grant," said Forbes, "and almost a week to go. We may do it yet."

❧ NINE ❧

Celia sat in a deck chair with the blue water of the Bay of Islands lapping against the landing stage. It was early afternoon. Lucy and the baby were both asleep. Muriel was indoors writing letters. Out in the bay, sailing dinghies and pleasure launches scudded about through the maze of islands. Seagulls with coral pink legs wheeled overhead. Near the far shore three naval ships whose crews were to take part in tomorrow's celebration were dressed overall with bunting. Behind them the huge lawn in front of the Treaty House, where the controversial agreement wa signed in 1840, sloped gently towards the water. It was hard to believe that an evening's jollification in this peaceful setting would be the signal for terrorists to kill a hostage.

"Of course I shall go," Muriel had said over breakfast. "It's their National Day. I quite see that they can't cancel it because of what these people are threatening to do to Bertie, and I must show them that

I support them in their decision. Father always used to say that one must never let private grief interfere with public duty.''

Celia decided that Muriel must be either very brave or very insensitive. The whole country was tense with nerves about the kidnapping and death threat, and the papers, after ignoring the whole subject for weeks, were full of nothing else. This was partly Forbes' doing. Photos of the five known terrorists were everywhere, on posters and handbills headed "Have you seen these men?" The public was co-operating, reports of sightings were coming in all the time and being investigated by detectives. So far they had all proved to be false alarms or inconclusive.

A launch curved in to the landing stage and Forbes stepped out, looking as black as a thundercloud. "Where's Lady Albert?"

"Inside, writing letters," said Celia.

"Please try to persuade her to stay away tomorrow."

"I have already, it's no good."

"She must. A new possibility has opened up that she'd find very distressing."

"Tell me."

"I was wrong. I calculated that we'd have several more kidnappings. One person shot in Auckland and left for us to find in the boot of a stolen car wouldn't be very impressive."

Celia agreed. An offstage killing miles away would not have maximum impact. What was needed was a resounding piece of terrorist theatre on the spot of Waitangi.

"And I'm afraid they're going to get it," said

Forbes grimly. He explained that Bob Perrin, one of the spoilt rich boys identified by Andy's parents in Remuera, had a pilot's license, a fact which had not rung an alarm bell with the policeman to whom it was mentioned casually by the Perrin family. Forbes heard about it only two days later and realized at once what it might mean.

"He could have bought a light aircraft months ago when they were planning this, and hidden it away ready for tomorrow. We've looked everywhere the light plane could take off. We're still looking."

"But can't the air force deal with that?" Celia asked. "In the last resort, I suppose they could shoot it down."

"With a live hostage in it, that they proposed to dump on the lawn at Waitangi under the Governor-General's nose?"

It was six in the evening. The audience for the Waitangi Day ceremony was assembling. The car that Forbes had organized for Muriel and Celia inched its way through a mass of humanity on foot, heading for the grounds of the Treaty House. Were there morbid sightseers among them? Hard to tell, it looked like an ordinary holiday crowd, with rugs to sit on and children eating ice cream.

Muriel was pale but astonishingly calm. Celia had not told her what she and Forbes feared. If it happened it would be an appalling shock for her. But imagining it for 24 hours beforehand would make it even worse.

The protest demonstration had been halted by the police halfway up the drive. It was surprisingly small, a few dozen people holding up placards denouncing the Treaty and shouting occasional slogans at passers-by on their way to the ceremony. Perhaps sympathizers had stayed away because joining it could be interpreted as support for terrorism. The police must have expected a much larger demonstration, their massive cordon of muscular men in full riot gear could have handled a violent mob ten times the size.

The car deposited Muriel and Celia at the entrance, guarded by more police. Photographers crowded round, and a woman darted forward to present Muriel with a small bunch of flowers as a token of sympathy. They moved forward into the neat little garden surrounding the Treaty House, one-storey, wooden, built in a graceful Regency style and painted cream. It has been the modest home of New Zealand's first Governor, and was now a carefully preserved historical relic. On their way through the little museum inside the building they passed Forbes, who muttered "no news, I'm sorry", as they went out on the far side into a roped-off area of lawn reserved for the diplomatic corps and distinguished guests. The concert party of Maori singers and dancers faced them across the lawn in traditional costume, a long line of men and women in brown and white and red, with the evening beauty of the Bay of Islands as background.

The Governor-General arrived. The ceremony began with a performance in which the leader of the concert party leaped about in front of him shouting in pretended defiance and anger, and finally laid a stick on the ground which Maori tradition required him to pick up as a sign that he had come in peace and friendship. After a prayer and a speech of welcome, the men of the concert party danced with proud, well-drilled grace, and the women sang in a haunting close harmony which Celia found very sad.

Beside her Muriel stirred in her chair. "They say that Waitangi means 'Waters of Mourning' in Maori," she murmured. It was the first time she had spoken since they arrived.

The next song was more cheerful. The women swung their *pois** in time with the music, making an intricate, dazzling pattern running down the whole line. Celia listened with half an ear and no enjoyment, and wondered if she would hear the drone of an aircraft above the music.

Meanwhile all over New Zealand policemen went on investigating reports from the public of suspicious behaviour. They had been doing so all day, and there was no reason for stopping because the Waitangi celebration had begun. Most reports came from the Auckland area, but a yacht which had behaved oddly in Whangarei harbour proved to contain five people engaged in sexual practices which astonished even the hardened constabulary. In the far north another report had come in. A bird watcher hidden in the dunes had been ranging with his binoculars over Parengarenga harbour, a deserted bay remarkable only as a source of white silicone sand for optical glass-making and normally deserted, except by bar-tailed godwits when they assembled there for the annual migration to Siberia and Alaska. According to the birdwatcher, a sea-going yacht had come into the bay and two men had attempted to transfer a third, who seemed to be unconscious, into a dinghy. After difficulties in which the dinghy narrowly escaped being capsized, they

*A *poi* is a white cotton ball on the end of a short string.

managed to bring him ashore, where he was loaded into a beach buggy which had driven through a gap in the dunes on to the deserted shore.

In the police station at Te Kao, this report was taken very seriously. Parengarenga harbour was only five miles from Ninety Mile Beach on the far side of the island. Ninety Mile Beach had been used for attempts on the world land speed record and a light aircraft could land and take off there at low tide. The instructions were to follow up urgently any hint that an aircraft might be involved. It might be too late, but it was worth whistling up a police helicopter to have a look.

At Waitangi, the concert pursued its course. Dusk was creeping down and Celia, tense with anxiety, was beginning to have had quite enough singing in a language and convention she did not understand. Then it came, the sound she had dreaded. Not just the drone of a light aircraft, but a huge noise from behind the trees to the north. Two navy helicopters came in sight flying low. A light aircraft, painted gaily in red and white, hurtled along between them. The helicopters were making lunges at it, like birds mobbing an intruder into their nest territory, in an attempt to make it change course. But the pilot took no notice and flew on steadily till he was directly over the open square of lawn between the distinguished visitors' enclosure and the line of singing Maoris. The door of the aircraft opened. Something was thrown out which resolved itself into a mass of disorganized, whirling limbs. It hurtled to the ground, and Muriel stood up and began to scream.

*   *   *

Twenty minutes earlier, Bazzer had been driving the beach buggy when Andy first spotted the police helicopter, flying low to take a close look at vehicles on the road leading up to the lighthouse at New Zealand's northernmost point. Any doubt about what it was looking for vanished when it made a low pass over the yacht riding at anchor in Parengarenga Harbour. Finding no one aboard, it began circling over the dunes, looking for the beach buggy. It would be spotted almost at once.

"Trouble," said Bazzer as the helicopter dived towards them. "Shoot him and shove him overboard and let's get out of here."

Bertie was still very drowsy from the effect of the sleeping pills. Andy pulled the trigger, then heaved Bertie's dead weight over the tailboard, ripping him free when his waistband caught on the number plate. The beach buggy sped on.

"Hijack a car on the road?" he suggested.

But there was only one road south down the narrow promontory. There would be road blocks. There was no hope of escape by land. But Bob Perrin would be landing the plane any moment now on Ninety Mile Beach, ready to take Bertie on board and dump him at Waitangi. Change of plan, Bazzer decided. Bob would have to fly him and Andy to safety instead; if they could get to it before the police helicopter did.

"You're sure he's dead?" Bazzer shouted as the beach buggy bounced among the dunes.

"I didn't aim at him."

"Why the hell not?"

"I couldn't bring myself to."

The helicopter landed 20 yards ahead. The policemen in it were armed, and shouted a summons to surrender.

Bob Perrin heaved the dummy out of the cabin door over Waitangi and flew on. He had seen the police helicopter swoop down like a hawk on the beach buggy, and realized at once that there was no point in landing on Ninety Mile Beach. Nothing could be done for Bazzer and Andy, and there would be no Bertie to drop overboard at Waitangi. This disappointed him for he was not a pleasant young man, and was destined to stand trial a few years later for half murdering a prostitute in Sydney. He would have quite enjoyed dumping a live victim on that ridiculously pompous jamboree. Having turned back south, he decided to go there anyway. A dummy was not a satisfactory substitute for Bertie, but it was better than nothing, and he had managed to improvise one out of his own sweater and trousers, stuffed with the two life jackets carried in the plane. At least it had given everyone a fright. To that extent it was valid terrorist theatre.

The two helicopters were still jostling him, but he had reckoned on that. He strapped on his parachute and set the controls for the plane to fly on out to sea till it ran out of fuel. It was dark now, if he parachuted down into one of the Auckland public parks he could be in the crowded streets long before the police net closed round him. Minus his trousers, he would have to pretend to be jogging.

At Te Kao police station Bazzer and Andy were waiting to be charged. "You should have killed him," said Bazzer.

"When it came to the point I couldn't."

"I could have, because he killed Rosie." After a moment Bazzer added: "They say killing people only upsets you the first time. After that you can kill people you don't hate and it doesn't worry you at all."

At Waitangi a deep moan of shock had come from the crowd as the horrifying object thumped down on the lawn. Policemen and stretcher bearers rushed forward and crowded round the spot, blocking the view. When a policemen held it up for all to see that it was a dummy, the moan changed to a vast laugh, but of relief, not of amusement. For a moment several thousand people had believed that they were watching a man being killed as an act of political terrorism and outrage. They had felt instinctively that once such a thing had happened New Zealand would never be quite the same again.

The long evening's programme was coming to an end. A Maori clergyman began reciting a prayer. "For the faithful observance of the Treaty of Waitangi", written by a much-loved former Governor-General: "Oh God, who in Thy beneficent wisdom in the year one thousand eight hundred and forty ordained that strife and bloodshed between races and tribes in this territory should cease and that the inhabitants of these islands should be knit together as one people under the British Crown, grant that the sacred compact may be faithfully and honourably kept for all time to come . . ."

Muriel was already on her way to Te Kao to be reunited with Bertie, who was unharmed except for a non-lethal overdose of sleeping pills and some bruises. It had fallen to Forbes to tell her that Bazzer's first act on arriving at the police station had been to produce a statement signed by Bertie confessing to the accidental shooting of Rose Murphy. He would have to stand trial for manslaughter. "Then I shall stay here, Celia, and visit him in prison," she said. "I shall like that, people here don't talk too fast and make me feel stupid."

As soon as Celia could find a telephone she rang Hermione to tell her that Bertie was safe. But as usual, it was Hermione who got in the first word.

"Celia dear, I've been meaning to ring you all day. Splendid news, you remember the naked marble gentleman at the top of the East Staircase? We've always assumed that he was run-of-the-mill eighteenth century, but it turns out that he's pukka Graeco-Roman and worth a bomb, and he comes from my side of the family so we can sell him without anyone's signature. I hope we haven't given you too much trouble and of course we'll pay your expenses as we said we would, but you needn't bother about Bertie anymore."

ABOUT THE AUTHOR

John Sherwood is a well-known British mystery writer whose books include GREEN TRIGGER FINGERS; DEATH AT THE BBC; THE DISAPPEARANCE OF DR. BRUDERSTEIN; MR. BLESSINGTON'S PLOT; AMBUSH OF ANATOL; and others. He lives in Kent, in the south of England.

MURDER... MAYHEM... MYSTERY...

From Ballantine

Available at your bookstore or use this coupon.

___**DEATH IN A TENURED POSITION**, Amanda Cross   32950   2.95
The country's most prestigious university faces a scandal guaranteed to mar its perfect reputation.

___**THE JAMES JOYCE MURDER**, Amanda Cross   33141   2.95
Mary Bradford had many enemies indeed, and one of them hated her enough to shoot her...but who?

___**GRAVE ERROR**, Stephen Greenleaf   30188   2.50
The wife of a leading consumer activist is afraid her husband may be killed or blackmailed.

___**DEATH BED**, Stephen Greenleaf   32742   2.95
A typical missing persons case becomes woven with murder, kidnapping, disappearances and ends with a final gruesome twist.

___**THE OUTSIDE MAN**, Richard North Patterson   30020   2.50
The hot and steamy South inhabited by genteel wealthy people who sometimes have to murder to protect what is theirs.

BB   **BALLANTINE MAIL SALES**
      Dept. TA, 201 E. 50th St., New York, N.Y. 10022

Please send me the BALLANTINE or DEL REY BOOKS I have checked above. I am enclosing $.................(add 50¢ per copy to cover postage and handling). Send check or money order—no cash or C.O.D.'s please. Prices and numbers are subject to change without notice. Valid in U.S. only. All orders are subject to availability of books.

Name_____

Address_____

City_____State_____Zip Code_____

Allow at least 4 weeks for delivery.

Attention Mystery and Suspense Fans

Do you want to complete your collection of mystery and suspense stories by some of your favorite authors? John D. MacDonald, Helen MacInnes, Dick Francis, Amanda Cross, Ruth Rendell, Alistar MacLean, Erle Stanley Gardner, Cornell Woolrich, among many others, are included in Ballantine/Fawcett's new Mystery Brochure.

For your FREE Mystery Brochure, fill in the coupon below and mail it to:

**Ballantine/Fawcett Books
Education Department — MB
201 East 50th Street
New York, NY 10022**

Name_____

Address_____

City_____State_____Zip_____

12   TA-94